T0072507

BEAUTIFUL IS LOVE

A WORK OF FICTION

BY: AMY RHEA HARRISON

MANUSCRIPT AND COPY EDITOR:
GLENDA JORGENSEN

BOOK-COVER DESIGN:
AMY RHEA HARRISON AND ASSOCIATES

PROOFREADERS:
MOLLY ADAMS, GLENDA JORGENSEN,
DOUG HARRISON, JESSICA MITCHELL

authorHOUSE®

AuthorHouse™ LLC
1663 Liberty Drive
Bloomington, IN 47403
www.authorhouse.com
Phone: 1-800-839-8640

© 2013, 2014 Amy Rhea Harrison. All rights reserved.
Cover Design Copyright: 2014 Amy Rhea Harrison

http://www.beautifulislove.com
http://www.amyrheaharrison.com

No part of this book may be reproduced, stored in a retrieval system, or
transmitted by any means without the written permission of the author.

Published by AuthorHouse 04/30/2014

ISBN: 978-1-4969-1004-2 (sc)
ISBN: 978-1-4969-1003-5 (e)

Library of Congress Control Number: 2014907993

Any people depicted in stock imagery provided by Thinkstock are models,
and such images are being used for illustrative purposes only.
Certain stock imagery © Thinkstock.

This book is printed on acid-free paper.

Because of the dynamic nature of the Internet, any web addresses or links contained in
this book may have changed since publication and may no longer be valid. The views
expressed in this work are solely those of the author and do not necessarily reflect the
views of the publisher, and the publisher hereby disclaims any responsibility for them.

"Beautiful Is Love" is a work of fiction. Some places, cities, and states named in this book, do
exist and are used solely as an inspiration for this storyline. Remaining places, all names of
people, events, or time-lines, are a result of the author's imagination, and any incidents that
resemble any living or dead person, or place & history, are entirely coincidental. Contents
of this book contain adult language, political topics &/or phrases, and sexual situations."

Contents

Chapter 1   Christmas With Dad 1

Chapter 2   Jacob & Naomi Willem 7

Chapter 3   Home Early 11

Chapter 4   Dinner 15

Chapter 5   Another Late Night..17

Chapter 6   Emergency At The Pass 20

Chapter 7   Crione Agency 25

Chapter 8   Didn't Call For Small Talk 29

Chapter 9   911 31

Chapter 10   Cambridge.. 34

Chapter 11   Bad Day.. 39

Chapter 12   Too Far 41

Chapter 13   Not Just An Engineer 44

Chapter 14   Another Explosion 48

Chapter 15   Inn At The E.R... 54

Chapter 16   Sever Ties 63

Chapter 17   Omaha 67

Chapter 18   Take Care of Her 70

Chapter 19   Let Me Explain... 73

Chapter 20   Sick of It 77

Chapter 21   Tall Man.. 81

Chapter 22   Bloody Hands... 86

Chapter 23   Like Father Like Son.. 92

Chapter 24   Low Down.. 96

Chapter 25   The Funeral.. 102

Chapter 26   Nothing More 106
Chapter 27   Hero Irene 112
Chapter 28   Gallery Event, Two Weeks Later 117
Chapter 29   Discovery 121
Chapter 30   No Hold 128
Chapter 31   Burned Out 131
Chapter 32   Freedom Has A Cost 133
Chapter 33   Beautiful Is Love 137

Author's Introduction:

Amy Rhea Harrison, born in California, moved to the State of New Mexico for eleven years where she met her companion in life. They now live near Arlington, Washington.

She was inspired to write this book on a sleepless night at a rented cabin in the mountains near OSO and Darrington, WA. After hearing unfamiliar explosion-like sounds in the mountains and fighter-jets flying overhead, she sat at her desk during a rainy and cold night in the late of May, 2011, and began to write the story of Jacob & Naomi Willem, in her first [intended to be] published fictional novel, Titled: Beautiful Is Love.

Author's note:

Keeping in mind as Shakespeare wrote, "What is past is prologue," Amy Rhea Harrison invites you to continue to the Preface section of this book, so that you may develop an understanding of who Jacob and Naomi Willem are, and how love plays such a strong factor in this story of their chaotic journey in life.

Beautiful is love, as sunrise is to daylight.
The equation does not calculate correctly the other way
around, as there is no daylight without a sunrise:
One part of the equation.
Love being compiled of so many different components.
Scary is love. Vulnerability is love. Giving is love. Forgiveness is
love. Compassion is love. Faith is love. Unconditional is love.

Yes, beautiful is love.
It can carry you through hardships or sink the ship itself.

-Amy Rhea Harrison

I dedicate this book:

To my pillar & love in life, Doug Harrison: for your inventive help, inspiration, wit, and encouragement throughout this project

To my mother: for your unconditional love, expertise, & support.

. . . . and, to Molly, my fish: What else can I say? You're my butterfly.

This life would not be complete without each of you as a part of it!

PREFACE

On November 3rd, 1970, Irene O'Brien gave birth to her only child, a new baby girl she had birthed, and named Naomi Joy O'Brien. In the middle of the night during Irene's first trimester, her husband Gary left without a word and to never return. Irene, having grown up in an abusive household throughout childhood, had escaped her home at fifteen years of age after a near death beating from her own father. She quickly grew accustomed to being independent, self-sufficient, and carried with her a deep bitterness towards men in general. She couldn't help but worry now that her daughter would face hurt and hardships in her life, and vowed to be the best parent to this new life she brought into this world.

When Irene stepped through the doors of her small apartment in Omaha, Nebraska, she felt desperate to keep Naomi safe from all harm. She bathed her new baby, and nursed her while rocking her to sleep. As she laid Naomi in her bassinet, Irene whispered, "It's just me and you baby," while caressing her infant's soft skin. "You can forgive, but never forget, my daughter. Never ever forget. This world is dark and cold, full of useless men, but you are my new light, and purpose. I will protect you. That I promise! I love you."

It was 1983 when Naomi O'Brien came home from her last day of school in junior high. She walked in the house to find her mother, Irene, sitting at the piano, sobbing. Irene sat Naomi down next to her and told her that her father, whom Naomi had never met even once in her life, had died, and that he had named Naomi in his Will. Her mother explained that when Naomi graduated from high school, she would receive a large settlement of money but she was required to complete college; any college of her choice. Naomi felt emotionless about the information, not sure what to think about any of it, and didn't care about the money because it would never replace the father she never had. Feeling wise beyond her years, she told her mother that for all she cared, this was a sure way to seal the deal that she would never go to college; simply out of principle. A factor she would realize as an adult in debt just how foolish a decision that was. "Your stubbornness is your passion," her mother would always say.

It was the end of her 8th grade year, and she already missed her best friend. Naomi let her mind wander to the end of summer, and grew excited to start high school so she and her best friend, Rose Carson, could be freshmen together at the same school again. They had been in the same school every year except this one when Rose's mom and step-dad moved to the other side of town of Omaha, which is where the only high school was located at the time in their small town, Battle River, Nebraska.

She and Rose were inseparable, except during summer when Rose would go spend those weeks with her father in Seattle, WA. Every start of a new school year, Rose would fill Naomi's imagination with all the exciting stories she had from her summer stay; all of the eccentric people and amazing places Rose had seen in Seattle. Rose's favorite place was Bell City, and the downtown plaza. Her dad would let her go there every day for as long as she wanted until he was home from work. Naomi was mesmerized by Rose's stories of the ocean, boats, tall buildings called high rises, the outside grocery stores and markets, old film festivals, local musicians serenading the streets, and all the artsy people. She vowed to experience life fully when she was older.

Naomi loved to draw, and was infatuated with painting. She didn't actually have the opportunity to paint until high school during her art class, where the supplies and paints were free. She soon found that she was a pure natural. Naomi and Rose's favorite hangout in their home town was at *Old Market Omaha, which was the premier arts and entertainment district downtown. This was Naomi's main influence for her passion of art, and it was where she met a fine looking boy named Jacob Willem, her senior year in high school.

During the summer of 1986 the Willems moved their large family of seven, including their son, Jacob, from Irving, Texas, to Omaha, Nebraska, for Richard's work as an industrial scientist. He had retired several years before providing his services to country as an acclaimed Military Scientist. Jacob was optimistic about the change. His mother always called him the glue in their family, always trying to make peace between his siblings. He had the wit to fit, and no matter how gloomy anyone would be feeling, with Jacob around, suddenly all things were brighter. They had lived in the same house in Irving, Texas, all his life, so he was excited for a new experience. He loved science, and his dad's new employment opportunity was fascinating to him. All Jacob could think about was doing big things, going to college, and becoming a successful business man. He wanted to please his parents and God, and would often imagine situations where he was in charge, instructing a team of other scientists or engineers on details to complete their big project, always dressed professionally sharp as his father, Richard, always did in a crisp suit, straight shirt, and ironed necktie.

When Jacob saw Naomi through a window of a little gallery in Old Market Omaha, he thought, "Love at first sight." She wasn't at all what he was used to going steady with. He liked the short, dark haired girls, that had a wild side, as being around girls like that brought out Jacob's feisty and dare devil characteristics; often finding himself in fist fights defending others. This girl though, "wow, this girl," he thought was pure and bright. She was nearly as tall as he was, reminded him of a beautiful and strong statue, and he couldn't help but to toss her a flirtatious eye and smile. Naomi saw him through that window, and confidently walked outside to meet this boy. She couldn't resist his charm either, appearing to be so innocent; she knew in that very moment: she was his girl for life.

After their senior year graduation in 1987, Rose Carson moved to Seattle to live with her father and go to nursing school. Jacob proposed to Naomi that summer. Of course, her mother was disapproving, and the Willems thought Jacob and Naomi were too young. Without the support from their parents, Jacob talked to Naomi again about his goals to go to MIT and that he still wanted to go to college. He told her they should wait to marry after their parents calmed down, but Naomi, feeling defiant, and afraid she would lose the love of her young life, told him, "no chance." Naomi stole money from her mom's purse even though she knew Jacob had his checking account that his parents religiously put money into monthly for him. They hopped on a bus in the middle of the night and eloped to Las Vegas, Nevada the following evening. They ran away to Cambridge, Massachusetts to move into their very own studio apartment. They were so excited. They had already decided they would tell their parents once they arrived there, so they continued their adventurous journey and called it the best summer of their lives.

The young Willems fresh out of high school, hitch hiked everywhere, stopping for a few days at a time, exploring the countryside together. They visited galleries and science museums, took photographs of interesting architecture, and made love every moment possible, and especially in the not so possible places. They talked about everything: money, goals, art, their parents, family, God, the real reason why Naomi refused to go the college (defying her dead father's inheritance), and the mistakes she wouldn't make when she had a child of her own. It was beautiful, their love, and they made a simple goal: finish College, get good jobs, buy a house, have a baby. They were in love, young, and married. Nothing could stop them, until only six months later when Naomi found out she was pregnant.

Rose decided to move to Cambridge to be closer to Naomi so she could be her midwife. Naomi eventually had a miscarriage, which was followed by her best friend becoming distant and withdrawn. Rose ended up moving back to Washington less than a year later, and Naomi fell into a deep depression. She didn't lift a paint brush for nearly a year.

Jacob's junior year of college had just begun when he was inundated with offers for employment in the U.S. military, with various special agencies, the top engineering team in France, and the Crione Agency. In March of 1991, a man named Frank Calister, President of Crione Agency, visited MIT to give a speech on the discovery of nuclear weapons. While there, he met with Jacob Willem, and informed him he had been tracking his scholastic achievements since day one that Jacob's attendance took effect at MIT. Mr. Calister knew every detail of Jacob's life, his wife, Naomi being an artist, and his father, Richard Willem's work history. Some people would be put off by such an invasion of privacy, but Jacob was impressed and flattered. A year later, Mr. Calister told Jacob about a top secret project he was considering Jacob to be head engineer of and a week after graduation he flew him in a private military style helicopter to the project site after only a short yet confidential briefing. Jacob accepted the job.

Naomi supported Jacob's decision. She had begun initiating her own at-home-business online, marketing her artwork and paintings. She was confident she could do that anywhere. Naomi began looking for homes to move into once Jacob was given the vicinity of the project site destination. She learned that they were moving only an hour away from where her once best friend, Rose, had moved to. It had been about two years since they'd seen each other; Naomi had flown to a town near Ballard, outside of Seattle, to visit Rose, and try to mend things. Instead she found herself on a journey of self-exploration, and a freedom she had never known before. She stayed there for weeks with a couple she met at a local art function. They took her in and welcomed her to their couch and home while she figured things out. They charged her a minimal weekly rent, which allowed Naomi the freedom to explore this new place. It felt like a completely different culture. She fell in love with the scenery, people, and experiences, and the time away from Jacob only reassured her of her love and devotion to him. Her wandering reminiscence brought her to their present situation, and she knew they could get through anything after everything they had already been through. "This will be perfect," she said aloud to herself.

After the summer of 1992, Jacob accepted that position with Crione Agency near Glacier Point Peak Pass outside of Darrington, WA, to be Head Engineer at a nuclear warhead facility, and life took its course. The young Willems were experiencing a new found love and devotion to one another. They laughed all of the time, and spent every rare moment together talking about everything except money and work. They were happy.

Fifteen years later, in 2007, Jacob grew ill. With work spiraling out of control, they quickly found themselves in a world of confusion, stacking medical bills, bloodied chaos, explosions, and dead bodies. Faced with illnesses that were followed with accidents, betrayal, and conspired-cover ups, they became proficient in telling lies.

Naomi questioned how they could ever remain together as she quickly felt the implications from a rapidly crumbling marriage. Despair took over her.

However, when Rose Carson came back into their lives, life as the Willems knew it had changed, and Naomi would do anything to fight to keep it. She knew she and Jacob loved one another, and it was a beautiful kind of love. Over the course of weeks to follow, their dedication to each other grew even more after learning the power of forgiveness.

Beautiful is love, even if it is questionable.

CHAPTER 1

CHRISTMAS WITH DAD

In the summer of 1985, certain names involved with research resulting after the *1945 Trinity Fireball in the U.S., as Military Scientists, were exposed after an unarmed civilian protest against nuclear weapons took place on the courthouse steps outside of Irving, Texas. A group of people against modern guerrilla warfare and the fight against baring arms found a purpose to fight for a right they were not familiar enough with to really do anything about, so they protested, a means for attention when avenues for resolve are unclear.

Media was frenzied over the display of passionate protestors, with their picket signs and painted faces, all posing and chanting against the right for armed civilians, and against a particular group of scientists, including Richard Willem, that had been "indirectly" hired by the U.S. government to hide the U.S. involvement with current day countries that had possession of nuclear weapons. There, of course, were no direct connections between the fight to bear arms, the Trinity Fireball, and a group of armed civilians supporting the *Nuclear Club, so protestors were soon looked at as ignorant; these were people that wanted to fight, wanted to stand for something they convinced themselves was for the better good, and took hold of any unfamiliar word and so called it their purpose. Fighting for a concept of cause with no examples to prove their point except a list of names, they were left being seen as a nuisance, and their point of argument was disregarded only after two long days of protest.

However, the leaking of the names of the said military scientists "not directly involved" with the U.S government, quickly led government officials' decision to sever their ties with their project to re-establish grounds of communication within the Nuclear Club, particularly France, who at the time had established their own research center for new avenues to store and transport nuclear warheads; and so the scientists were given the option to retire. Richard Willem accepted a position in Omaha, Nebraska, as an Industrial Scientist for a small research and development firm. That position was to take place in December that year.

As an Industrial Scientist, Richard Willem would be *applying science as the application of scientific knowledge transferred into a physical environment, which would include testing theoretical models using formal science, and solving practical problems using natural science.

He specialized in the *major aspect of industrial engineering, planning the layouts of factories, designing assembly lines, and other manufacturing paradigms. Richard would be working to perfect time management, fiduciary goals within the company, managing materials and energy, all through the design of operational logistics. He would be the consultant for efficiency expertise, plan complex distribution schemes through computer simulations, and organize discrete event simulation, along with using extensive mathematical tools and modeling. He would be the go-to man for all accounts and in charge of the new location for this research firm in Omaha.

On Christmas day, Richard drove home from work. He parked in the garage and sat for a moment holding a small neatly wrapped box in his hands. Inside this small box was his Christmas gift to his wife, Florence. He had it specially wrapped for her, a shimmering gold colored thick paper covered with glitter, and topped with a deep purple bow made from suede. He thought for several minutes about the job offer he accepted months ago, and how they would all be moving soon from their lifelong home in Irving, TX, to a place they had never been before, a small town outside of Omaha, NE.

When Richard walked inside their home through the garage door into the kitchen, Florence, his wife, and their seven children, of course home on this holiday, were preparing supper. Some of the children were stringing popcorn to place on the tree after Richard came home. Jacob, the second eldest, was helping his younger sisters with the last of ornaments and placing them on the tree amongst the small light blue and white bulbs. Christmas carolers were singing a distant "Oh Holy Night" down the block, and their voices seemed to echo through the neighborhood. Moments later, Richard and Florence brought in mugs of warm homemade cocoa with little marshmallows atop, into the living room where the children had gathered. All of the Willem children were crammed together, facing the back of the couch, knees on the sofa cushions, as their young faces peered out the big bay window; watching for the bundled up group of people wearing red, green, and white, decorated in holiday scarves, and carrying jingle bells while they sang as loud as they could, an array of Christmas carols.

When the phone rang, Jacob ran to answer. He called out, "Dad, it's your office!"

Richard walked back to the kitchen, his cool, calm, demeanor never seemingly affected, and picked up the mustard yellow colored receiver. He held it to his ear. The voice on the other end was not welcoming, and when Richard hung up, Jacob was still standing there, watching his father. "Son, I forgot your mom's gift at the office. I'll be right back, Okay? It's a surprise though, so Shh," he told Jacob with a smile and his index finger held to his lips.

"Okay, Dad!" Jacob smiled, and ran back into the living room. He sat next to his mom, smiling still. When Florence looked at him, she smiled too, and he took his mom's hand in his, and they sat together like that, watching the younger children, and waiting for the carolers to appear outside their front doorsteps.

When Richard pulled up to his office, the rear building appeared to be unaffected, but the main entrance was already engulfed in flames. Only two scientists from his research team had stayed to work, after all it was Christmas day, and they both stood outside, covered in black soot from the fire and smoke.

"What happened here?" Richard called out to one of the scientists as he walked over to them.

"Some kind of explosion, maybe a bomb, Richard. It had to have come from the mail room. It went off right after we hung up!" the man responded excitedly . . . obviously frightened.

"Did everyone get out safely?"

"Just us two left, Sir, and we're fine."

"Could you salvage any materials?" Richard asked the man.

"No, Sir . . . We couldn't get to them. We just ran out as quickly as we could. I . . . I'm sorry."

"That's alright. Why don't you two head home. Try to keep this under wraps the best you can, okay? No one needs to know what happened here."

"Yes, Sir."

The two scientists headed to their vehicles and Richard watched them drive away just as the Emergency Fire Response teams pulled up with their fire trucks and ambulance. The local police arrived about a minute later. They questioned Richard, and he lied, telling them he was working late, and had an accident in the research center, mixed the wrong chemicals together and it caused an explosion which set off the fire. Apologizing profusely, pretending to fear he would lose his job, the officers eventually sympathized for him and advised Richard go on home to his family. They told him they would call upon him if they had any further questions.

In agreement, Richard started to walk back towards his car. Looking around to see if anyone was watching him, which they were not, he ran to the entrance around back in the rear building. When he opened the door, he burned his hand on the copper doorknob, but knew he had to save the blueprints for all their research. They were the most important documents to salvage, and he knew he would need them to start his new project in Omaha. As Richard ran through the fire engulfed rooms, covering his mouth and nose from inhaling all the thick smoke, he came to his office. He stood there in shock as he watched through his clear glass paned walls, a room completely smothered in flames. "It's all in there," he said to himself, shaking his head back and forth, feeling desperate and suddenly unaware of the blanket of fire surrounding him.

Just then, the roof in the room next to where Richard was standing caved in, sending shards of glass, embers, and aflame wood beams, crashing down and rumbling the ground beneath him. Shaken, he turned to run back out of the building the way he had come in. As he reached the rear exit doors, he tripped over a fallen filing cabinet, and fell to the ground. A part of the ceiling came crashing down, and landed across his legs. Kicking the fiery embers off of him, he crawled as fast as he could, and pulled himself out from under the ceiling particles; he was out the door quickly, lying on the moist yellow grass beside the sidewalk outside the building, staring up at the flames. With minor burns on his hands and legs, he headed back to the emergency medical team to bandage his wounds. He was surprised no one questioned him, and so then calmly, yet quickly, walked to his car.

Richard drove home, not sure what to expect after all of this, and hoping the police would accept his story and not find the real cause of the fire.

Back home, Florence had pulled the turkey from the oven, and asked the kids if they knew where their father had sneaked off to. Jacob's little brother, several years younger than his near seventeen, had heard their dad's conversation with him, and spoke up, telling his mom, "Dad forgot your present at work, Mom!" Feeling proud of himself for telling, he gave her a big smile, and ran out of the kitchen. Jacob was still standing there with his mom. He and his sisters always helped with the stuffing and cranberry sauce, and his mom turned to Jacob saying, "I don't know why they always make them work on holidays—Especially a day like Christmas!"

"Gosh, Mom, I don't know why either, but you know, Dad said your present was supposed to be a surprise, so maybe you shouldn't say anything, you know . . . don't want to spoil it, right?" Jacob told Florence, with a wide grin, and half hug around her waist so she wouldn't drop the turkey. He was already taller than his mother, and yet that handsome young face, Florence could not get enough of. She placed the turkey on the counter, stood straight and looked up at him, smiling; she hugged him tight and said, "I just love you, Son!"

"Wow, something sure smells delicious in here!" Richard announced as he walked through the kitchen door from the garage once more.

"Richard!" Florence yelled, frightened by the sight of her husband, covered in soot, and hands wrapped in terrycloth. "What happened to you?"

"Oh, we had a little emergency at work. It's alright. Somehow a fire started, and I have some minor burns on my hands and my right leg. No biggie, Darling." Richard responded optimistically, not wanting to alarm any of his family any more than his appearance already was.

Florence ran over to him and stood staring at him, half mad, but mostly worried. She had a look of question written across her face but did not want to say too much in front of the children. Richard leaned forward, giving her a long kiss, and swooped her up off the floor into his arms, ignoring the pain in his hands; he told her, "Do you have any idea how much I love you, Mrs. Willem?"

Giggling like a school girl, Florence pushed herself back out of his arms. Richard held her shoulders softly as her feet found her balance. She gave him a sly smile; her faced still blushed, and waved the corner of her apron at the air in his direction. "Oh, you . . ." Florence replied, walking back towards the kitchen counter. "Well, why don't you go get washed up? Supper is nearly ready."

After Richard showered, his son, Jacob, and his older brother, helped their dad re-bandage his hands and leg. While the other kids watched in amazement, Richard told them some extravagant story of what had happened at his work. When Jacob finished, Richard gave them all a big smile, and announced "Let's open some presents!"

"Yay!"

"Woo-woo!"

"YES, I knew it!"

Cheers shouted from all the children as they ran down the hall towards the living room where the Christmas tree and presents sat, taunting their patience all day long.

Florence hollered out from the dining room, "Hold it! Supper first."

Sitting at the table, after Richard gave thanks in prayer for their family, and the lovely supper Florence had worked on all day, Jacob said, who had been excited about the idea of moving and fascinated about his dad's new career all along, said "Dad, tell us about your new job offer again!"

"First, I have something for your mom, Children." Richard handed Florence her gift.

The room was silent as they all watched their mother light up like an angel. She softly took the little box from Richards's bandaged hands and held it in both hands, so gently as though she was holding a new born bunny.

"What is it?" The oldest son asked.

"Ya', what is it, Mom?" said their youngest daughter.

"We'll open this later, in bed." Florence responded flirtatiously into Richard's ear, and she placed the small gift wrapped box in front of her plate by her wine glass, "later Children, now let's eat up before it gets cold!"

Chapter 2

Jacob & Naomi Willem

He woke that morning in early May of 2007 with Naomi at his side. She slept with her head at the opposite end of the bed, turned slightly on her side and stomach at the same time, caressing his muscular calves and thighs, giving soft kisses to his toes and ankles. Naomi loved Jacob with every ounce of energy in her bloodstream. He was her knight, her rescue when she didn't realize she was stranded.

Jacob Willem was tall and strong, his skin toned a sun kissed tea color, ocean blue eyes that lit up in the sun's rays a light green and gray . . . and those legs, she could stand him on his hands and hang hangers from those calves. He was intelligent, educated, well-mannered, loved his parents and God, had a fantastic wit and sense of humor about him, and he had his feisty side that she couldn't resist, almost a bad-boy charm: no doubt, hook, line, and sink. Yes, Jacob did it for her. He was Naomi's best friend, and several days later she would realize she had lost her life as she knew it to him.

Jacob moaned at the touch of Naomi stroking his legs and returned the gesture with a rubdown on her side and back only his hands could give. He knew Naomi couldn't resist his touch. She called his hands magical and that lit a surge inside of him that could not easily be extinguished.

As Jacob massaged Naomi's soft skin, he twisted slightly as he sat up to kiss the curve of Naomi's back. He whispered, "Good morning, Mrs. Willem, my joy."

Naomi smiled and returned the morning greeting. "How are you feeling, my love?"

Jacob smiled, stood, and in a slow motion, he leaned over Naomi to kiss her forehead; his silhouette, in front of the morning sun rays glistening through the curtains and darkness of their bedroom, encompassing her. Naomi could feel his warmth. She felt so much comfort from his presence.

Jacob didn't answer, and he knew she understood. Naomi watched him walk away from their bed, and around the corner, out of her sight. She missed him already. How pathetically wonderful, she thought.

There was an essence about Naomi that Jacob could not quite figure out. After all these years, he found her mystery essence still a fascinating draw to his appetite. She wasn't at all his type. He always seemed drawn to the feisty, outgoing and athletically fit type of woman. Women with dark straight hair that could be pulled away from her face to a predominately fashioned retro style. He loved those good'ol'girls with their rockabilly attitudes and flat bottomed shoes, the girl that could go fisticuffs' over a simple slurred word thrown her way. The girl he could wrap his arms around and her face would be engulfed in his masculine body and bold chest. The girl he could never take home to Mom.

Naomi was almost his height. When they hugged, her head would lean against his shoulder. She had wavy red hair that hung nearly to her waist, locks of curls often falling across her face. She had a curved figure of a succulent pear, deep green eyes that he often felt were looking straight into him; she was funny, book smart, an artist, and wise beyond her years. She had an innocence about her though, an angelic face and lips of a goddess. He remembered the day they met. Seeing her through a gallery window, she looked like a piece of art he had never seen before. She appeared before him as a magnificently strong statue, mysterious, charismatic, and endearing which is what made her so approachable. She was the most devoted and caring person he had ever known. Naomi was all passion, and had a temper to fit. He knew he would not ever want to cross it again. Jacob couldn't resist her.

He stood in the shower, feeding his sore bones a soothing hot flow of water. Thinking back on the times when he was a teenager and into his twenties, and how hard he was on his body. Boy, he missed those days, so careless, newly married, and yet he felt so free. He never thought that getting into fist fights, playing ball, roping cattle, and jumping from airplanes would do harm to him when he was only nearing forty. He hated his physical health at this stage in life, and regretted the pain he anticipated that the day would bring before he even left the solitude of his shower.

The hot water steamed the bathroom to the perfect thick air he loved. Fog clouded the mirrors so he couldn't see his reflection, and the moist air caressed his hurting skin. He didn't want to leave this place. He could have stayed in that shower for the rest of his life. He wanted Naomi badly, to feel inside of her, her warmth, and her moistness. He let his mind wander a moment, thinking of the amazing times they had in bed . . . and on the floor, and on the balcony, and in the kitchen, and that dingy bathroom in Las Vegas after they married. "Ooh, yes, Vegas . . ." he thought as a wide grin took control of his face; and in the car, that Vegas elevator, and their picnic table out front . . . frustration suddenly engulfed his thoughts as the realization of the present time in their lives took precedence, and how he hurt too badly. He wanted to stay there, in his sanctuary of solitude and hot moist air, and hoped Naomi would return to her slumber. He couldn't handle the thought of disappointing her, or disappointing himself.

Naomi, still lying in bed, messy covers wrapping themselves around and across her long legs and torso, and up across to hang off one shoulder; stretched long and wide, both legs and arms sprawled across the bed, until she felt a tingle in her head, almost as though she could faint. She breathed deep, in and out through her nose several times, until she felt the tingle fade away. She took a deep breath in, and exhaled as she sat up. All in one motion, Naomi found herself sitting on the bed with her legs crossed in front of her. She inhaled once more, lifting her arms high above her head, stretching her fingers to the ceiling, and exhaled as she brought her arms back down slowly in front of her, resting her hands on her bare feet. She curled her toes and hugged them tight inside of her fingers against her palms. She took another deep breath, in and out, slowly.

She set her feet on the ground beside the bed, whispering to herself, "Here we go."

Walking to the kitchen, she opened curtains and windows as she passed through the house. She put coffee on to brew. She wished Jacob enjoyed coffee. How nice it would be to share that time together, to be able to sit and talk over coffee together each morning, she often thought. She opened the cupboard and retrieved her daily doses of medicine for her asthma and the arthritis she was born with, and her herbal supplements, which her mother-in-law, Florence, had convinced her once many years ago, would increase her energy and focus. She tossed the dozen little pills in her mouth together in one swoop, and swallowed them down into her belly with a large glass of cool tap water. She loved the taste of their water. She thought about the *documentary, Tapped, she once saw about the role of the bottled water industry and its effects on our health, climate change, and pollution . . . she paused in thought and could picture the scene about plastic water bottles that circled the circumference of the earth in a years' time, and found herself frustrated because she couldn't remember the name of that particular documentary. "What a horrible sight," she murmured, enough litter to circle the globe in such a short amount of time. She was glad she didn't contribute to that consumption omitting mess, besides, "It's a waste of money," she mouthed silently. Shrugging her shoulders, she giggled a slight chuckle aloud at herself for talking to the air again.

"Just like my mom," she said aloud, shaking her head.

"What was that?" Jacob asked, as he walked into the kitchen.

"Ooh-nothing," Naomi waved the air, as if the wave excused her talking to herself. She wondered if she came across rudely just then, if Jacob thought she was actually talking to him. She couldn't stand the thought of hurting his feelings. "Stop analyzing every little detail already," Naomi said to herself. This time, quietly.

CHAPTER 3

HOME EARLY

It was a cool evening. The raindrops were hitting softly on the ground outside. All the windows were open in the house, and a slight breeze coddled the air inside. Dusk was nearing, so Naomi was glad to hear Jacob in the background already. "He's not usually home from work by this hour," she thought. "Must've been a good day, or a really bad one." She hoped for the good.

She had become accustom to not asking how his day was. Jacob was elusive about his work, never indulging too many details with Naomi. He told her it was for her safety. She didn't care about that. She just wanted him to be healthy and safe. He would talk to her about those things on his own time. They shared a deep connection with each other and both seemed to understand each other's silences. She would wait for him to get settled and unwind from his day.

Naomi could hear the flow of the river nearby. She was in her study painting, procrastinating finishing the budget. It would be tight this month. There hadn't been any purchases on her paintings for a few months. Jacob made a decent living, but with the two car payments, their mortgage, insurances, all the regular bills, and the stacking medical bills for Jacob, they depended on her income as well. Naomi blamed herself for not taking that money from her father; a man she had never met, whom her mother never spoke of except the day she told Naomi he had died and left her in his will with stipulations attached to the money, of course. "Maybe I should've gone to college, just for that money . . ." deep sigh, "I don't know." She wondered if the doctors would ever figure out what was wrong with Jacob. She missed him so much . . . feeling his body against hers, making love at any given moment. She sighed off all of those thoughts and continued painting, trying to clear her mind. The answers will come, she told herself. "I just need to get out there and market myself again," she muttered aloud.

There was a distant noise Naomi couldn't quite figure out. Maybe gunshots, she thought. Another. The sound grew louder as she heard the second and the third unfamiliar noise. The loud booms echoed through the valley, as she felt a slight vibration below her feet on their wooden floor. "That was no gunshot," she murmured.

Jacob poked his head into Naomi's office. He got a kick out of teasing her sometimes. She didn't like her space being called an office. She said it took the entire spark out of it. Jacob glanced over to where she normally sat at her desk when she was working at the computer. He was pleased to see Naomi standing in front of her easel with paint brush in hand. He would always tell her that he loved her art, but truthfully, he didn't quite understand it, or any art for that matter. He wasn't about to admit he didn't understand it either, as he knew from long ago that Naomi's weakest button to be pushed, was for her, in midst of all of her good intentions, was to feel misunderstood. Jacob was a black and white kind of guy, and he was okay with that. Naomi brought the romantic side out of him, and he loved her poetic rhythm as he watched her when she didn't know he was watching. "Damn, you're sexy," he thought.

"Did you feel that?" Jacob asked calmly not waiting for a response. "Felt like an explosion."

There were looming sounds coming from outside. They looked at each other, eyebrows halfcocked, both wondering the same thing.

"Well, what is that?" Naomi inquired matter of factually.

Jacob shrugged his shoulders, widened his eyes, raised his brows, and pouted his bottom lip out in a gesture to say he had no clue at all.

They walked to the back of the house to the sun room. Their three story home sat atop a hill, on a half-acre lot, surrounded by trees, with well-groomed landscaping. Naomi did the gardening herself, except the roses. Those were Jacob's babies. Gardening was Naomi's meditation time, her peace and quiet from everything else in the world. Jacob had his long showers and he jogged. She wished she could join him on those early morning runs, but she had never been much of a runner, considering her asthma.

The back deck from the sun room overlooked the river into the valley. Their backdrop was a giant mountain that was higher than they could see from inside the house. It was smothered with trees, and wilderness. Snow still blanketed the mountain even though it was spring. In the valley all the snow had melted weeks ago, and the spring scenery was quite different than that of the icy expression on the distant mountains.

Jacob opened the sliding glass door, stepping to the side for Naomi to have room to step out onto the deck first, and then followed straight behind her. He cusped the lower curve of her back and waist with his hand as they walked to the edge of the deck. She leaned her body naturally into his as they walked to the railing.

Leaning out as far as they could, hands perched on the redwood rail, shoulders flexed to extend their heads out like turtles stretching to eat, they could see a huge white cloud of smoke, maybe snow, Naomi thought. Perplexed at the sight of a giant teardrop of snow falling from the blue-gray sky, they were caught off guard when another loud boom shook their ground. This time, there was not a smoky snow cloud, but the ground shook so fiercely that they nearly lost their footing.

"Do you suppose that they're dynamiting to clear the avalanches again?" Naomi asked Jacob.

He shrugged and shook his head, "Must be."

"Honey, really, what do you think that is? I know it wasn't gun shots. I know that sound. You work near there. You must've heard something! This sound's different than the normal explosions we hear this time of year."

Jacob smirked towards Naomi, half rolling his eyes, the corner of his top lip curled up on one side, and calmly replied, "My joy, how the hell should I know what they are doing up there? For all I know, they are figuring out a way to forge a valley through the deadbeat texting teenagers that are loafing around on the couch instead of being productive citizens!"

Naomi glared at him, her eyes squinting in a way that says, "Don't push it, Buddy." She tossed him a sly smile, returning his sarcasm in a quiet manner, and turned to face the valley, allowing her mind to focus on the soothing melody from the ripples in the nearby river again.

"Smart ass," she pleasantly said out loud.

Jacob kissed Naomi's cheek, turned, and walked inside.

Uneasiness having taken over her, Naomi was frozen still in the moment, standing with her arms rested on the redwood deck railing, as she had a moment ago. She stared back out at the mountain and the big snow teardrop still slightly falling from the sky. She wondered as it dissipated, what in the world could be going on out there.

The phone's ringing disturbed Naomi's worry, and she headed back inside to her study. Jacob always answered the house phone. She had her business line in her study. It hadn't rung in weeks, and she didn't believe in mobile phones. Jacob was attached to his cell phone during the day, and had grown accustomed to the habitual action of turning off the cell when he came home from work. He had convinced Naomi into getting one several months ago when he started feeling sick, but the only time she used it was when he was at the hospital. She would make calls for him to his parents and a voice mail she would leave for his boss, Clint.

She heard Jacob hang up the receiver. She looked down the hall to see Jacob rustling with his jacket, and tearing off his tie. He tossed the tie over the back of the chair and ran his fingers through his hair. She watched him as he gently rubbed his brow with his fingers, and she wondered what the call was about. He did not see her standing in the hall.

"Everything alright?" she called out.

"Baby, I have to go to the office. I'll be back after a while."

So much for an early evening home together, Naomi thought. Oh-well. "Be careful my love. Should I make something for dinner?"

Jacob was out the door without offering an answer and Naomi watched him shut the door behind him without a glance her way.

CHAPTER 4

DINNER

Having been painting most of the day, the arthritis in Naomi's hands began to throb. She finished some final touch ups and cleaned her brushes.

*Queen Latifah's, The Dana Owens Album, played in the background. As the soul filled album delivered vocals of California Dreamin', Naomi was sent into a passion induced coma, mind drifting to times when she had chased away her worries with laughter; easier times, the freedom she felt as a young woman, so innocent to the world's decay. She felt warmth of liquid velvet take over her, closing her eyes, taking in a moment of this suspended reality. Sitting at her desk, she opened her eyes, seeing clearly now; eyes of an eagle, she stared out, welcoming the cool breeze's arrival, surpassing her pain, in her comfy-wear, and fuzzy socks, enjoying the peace of the river's harmony with the *Queen singing along; she called on her creative juices to return to her by coffee-cup's end, for a productive day ahead.

Naomi sat up straight, slowly arched her back and stretched her arms out long and wide, feeling her fingertips extend long. She ignored the pain of her arthritis, allowing the tingle to rejuvenate her bones. Taking in a deep breath, stretching even farther, in comfort she released her breath, focus finding her at last. She turned on her computer, and began to research online for any available gallery space. She worked the details for her next show and made all the necessary calls. "Well, that didn't take as long as I thought it would," she said admiringly to herself.

Satisfied, she let out a sigh of relief, one step of the project now done. The gallery show was scheduled; only three weeks out though, so Naomi knew she had her work cut out for her. With the paintings in the attic, and the one she finished today, she knew she needed at least four more pieces to complete her display at this gallery event. What audience she would target, she wondered. Should she stick to her mystical acrylic themes, or go more abstract? She'd been anticipating being able to try out her new oil set, to create a portfolio of still-life and tangibles, but was nervous about delving into something new now that she had a show booked. "Save that for the next project!" she whispered under her breath.

Deciding to stick to what she knew best, she poured herself back into her project, revisiting the thickness of the familiar acrylics. Mixing the blues with the reds, and yellows with greens, creating new shades she did not usually use. Darker, she thought. Her left hand holding her pallet of paints, and her right holding her brush, she closed her eyes and took in a deep breath, exhaling slowly, waking up her imagination. She could feel her soul igniting and before she realized it, she began sending long strokes of bold, dark, shades onto the blank canvas. The shapes found themselves as her hands took over for her mind, eyes, and soul.

A soothing rush took over Naomi. She found herself in a trance, naturally expressing her emotion and worry and desires into her art. She loved that feeling. Hovering above herself, feeling suspended, and able to release her pent up anxiety and worries. Here, she was free. Here, she felt like herself again. She hadn't realized until that moment that she was missing a part of herself, the girl she had found in Ballard with a nice couple that took her in for those weeks she was away from Jacob so many years ago. What was missing, she wondered. There was a deep quiver within her stomach, and an ache she couldn't recognize at first. "Dinner!" she proclaimed aloud. She had forgotten all about making dinner.

It seemed like hours had gone by. Naomi stood back, acknowledging she had completed two new paintings, making that three for the day. "I only need one more," she announced, and decided she would complete final touches the following day. Realizing she was starving, she wondered if she had eaten today. Promptly, she answered aloud, in an exclamation as though someone else were reminding her, "Yes, you had a bowl of fruit and granola early this morning with your coffee on the deck."

Sighing, Naomi looked at the clock. It was 10:00pm. Why wasn't Jacob home yet, she wondered.

Walking from her study, she grabbed her keys and pocket book, and headed out the door. "Chinese sounds good!"

CHAPTER 5

ANOTHER LATE NIGHT

Jacob phoned the house. He didn't expect Naomi to answer, and she didn't. It was nearly 10:30pm already. He'd leave her a message on the answering machine, he justified to himself.

After the sixth ring, the machine picked up, instructing callers to leave their message after the tone. He waited for the beep. Jacob could hear his own voice telling Naomi a lie. His shirt felt tight on his neck. Tugging slightly on one side of the shirt, he kinked his neck, cleared his throat, loosened another button, and continued on, speaking slowly into the receiver.

"My joy, Darling, I am sorry I won't be home for dinner. Don't worry about me; I'll eat here at the office. There's been an emergency in the development room, and I'm afraid we'll be here all night cleaning up this mess. Clint is really pissed and insists I take care of all the details. I really am sorry, my love." That part was true, he thought to himself. "Another late night. I'll explain later, I swear." His voice drifted, "I'll see you in the morning." Pausing, Jacob wondered if Naomi would hear the nervous rambling in his voice. "Sorry, I'm not feeling well," he added, "I miss you."

He closed his cell phone, and slipped it into his slacks pocket. Cupping his hands firmly together in front of him, he arched his shoulders, and headed inside the tunnel. "This is going to be a long night."

When Naomi returned home with dinner, she was surprised Jacob was still not home yet. She looked at her granddaddy's old chiming clock on the wall. It read 11:17pm. "You're never this late," she said aloud to Jacob as if he were in the room with her. Walking through to the kitchen, she set the bag of Chinese food on the center island counter, dropping her keys and pocket book along with the bags. The crinkling sounds from the paper grocery bags seemed piercingly loud. Noticeable silence appeared. She lifted the laptop; they kept there on the kitchen counter, to open and sent Jacob a quick email.

She typed:

"My love, I hope all is well. Sure do miss you. Got Chinese. Your favorite! Shoot me an email when you get this so I know you're alive, or call the study. Just kidding. Not about the email part. Do that.

PS. I have a show booked for the end of the month, just in time to get some extra money in. So, stop working so hard, and come home to me.

I love you,

Your joy"

She closed her laptop, and walked through the house closing all the windows and curtains. Tired and no longer hungry, she put the Chinese food still wrapped tightly in its paper bags, in the oven to keep warm. "He'll have an appetite when he gets home," she said. Her mind drifted to a wonderland, curious what Jacob was doing this very moment, imagining him at his desk, shirt unbuttoned, listening to his Bob Dylan CD play in the background, and rushing through paperwork to fix whatever error he had missed before he left for the day. "Too bad, must be a bad day," she confessed to the air filled room.

She flicked on the TV when she lay in bed just in time for the late night news. A newsflash appeared on the screen: Glacier Mount Peak Road exit from HWY 9 has been closed for the night. Unexpected delays. Advisory to seek alternate routes. (That's ridiculous, she thought, there are no 'alternate routes' to our place from Jacob's office). The news anchor flashed her camera across the ocean of traffic lights then back onto herself, her name edited in print in the corner of the screen, "Rachelle Wong, News Station 7, Reporting Live." No chance Jacob is getting through that. Knowing him, he'll pull the truck to the side of the road and sleep a bit. Naomi wondered what happened to the camera man. Sick of the TV already, she pointed the remote and hit "power-all" to turn everything off.

Not able to sleep and feeling restless, she slid out of bed and headed to her study. She moved the mouse for her computer with a slight bump of her finger, and refreshed her email. Nothing. Jacob hadn't responded. He was probably stuck in that awful traffic. She called his cell. It went straight to his voice mail. There was no answer on his office line either. She hung up just as another explosion illuminated the night sky and vibrated her floor. Pulling the curtain aside, not able to see anything beyond the silhouette of the mountain, she felt the chill from the cold window glass panes. It shot across her forearms and up her spine, sending goose bumps across her skin as if her freckles were playing connect the dots with her pores. She let the drapery fall back in to place, and she picked up her paint brushes.

"Yes, it must be a bad day."

CHAPTER 6

EMERGENCY
AT THE PASS

Jacob hurried out the door, down the steps to the driveway, fumbling for his keys on the way to his truck. He jumped in his old Dodge RAM 2500 diesel, turned the key to start the engine, not waiting for the glow plugs to warm up. He was in a hurry, and blazed out of the driveway down through the curvy mountain roads that led to Glacier Mount Peak Road, where he turned left through a red light, and stepped on the gas to HWY 9. He didn't stop for the red light there either, thinking to himself, I better slow down. "Get a grip, man," he said to himself. This was no time to lose control.

He passed the exit he would normally take to his office, and thought about calling Naomi. "That will have to wait." He accelerated to just above 90 MPH, and ten minutes later, took a sharp turn on the exit for Glacier Point Peak Road towards his work site outside of Darrington, Washington. He passed a news van going the opposite direction. "Strange. How'd they make it through our block off?" he wondered aloud. Looking through his rear view mirror, he saw the news van make a sharp right turn onto a private road. Shrugging it off, figuring it must be a coincidence, Jacob continued on. A few blocks up the road were an unusually high number of those Lable'ist semi-trucks, painted black. They were all headed down from the accident at Glacier Point Peak Pass.

In the meantime, other local news crews were heading in the direction of the accident dispatched by local police and fire response units. Ahead somewhere this had caused HWY 9 to a near standstill, and many of them were not able to get through. Reporter, Rachelle Wong, her cameraman, Steve Maders, and their sound guy, Joe Stanley, with Channel 7 were almost to the traffic site when Joe got the call from their supervisor, Bob Milson, to go check out the noise at the mountain.

"We're getting a ton of calls here about all the explosions out there. Go find out what you can and report back to me," Bob told Joe Stanley. "I want footage of the traffic for tonight, too, so don't leave without it or I'll have your jobs!" he continued.

"Such a prick," Joe announced after hanging up his cellular phone.

The crew of three wasn't exactly sure where to go and quickly found themselves lost, so they gave up and began to descend back down the curvy mountain road towards the traffic below. When they saw a Dodge truck passing them, Rachelle said to Steve, who was driving, "Quick, follow that guy!" pointing at Jacob's truck flying passed them.

Staying as far back as they could but still able to see Jacob's tail lights in the evening dusk setting quickly, they saw a long, almost train like, line of big Lable'ist trucks coming the opposite direction. Watching each one as they passed quickly by, Rachelle saw the last truck pull off onto a side road hardly noticeable to public. "Flip a bitch, Steve, follow that guy!" Rachelle said excitedly while smacking his arm over and over. "Alright, alright," he responded unamused, waving his arm back as though she were a fly he was waving off his face. He slowed quickly, making a three point U-turn in the middle of the two lane mountain road.

When Jacob arrived at the pass, he stumbled onto the site, shirt half tucked, still trying to gather himself, gather his thoughts, and any sign that would point to what went wrong. In his head, he kept hearing the words the dispatcher blurted out over the phone, "Emergency at the pass. Code red. Borgam expects you there ASAP."

There was dismay every which way he looked, smoke steaming out the opening to the tunnel at the mountain's entrance. The noise was so fierce he couldn't make sense of it. Everyone's mouths were moving, so he could see that people were talking, but he couldn't make out what anyone was saying. Large camouflaged trucks were on site, tarps tossed over heaping piles of who knows what, smoke still hissing off the dirt's ground now black from whatever had been burned away, and there were men in uniform sitting on edges of large rocks, holding bandages to their bloodied heads, legs, and shoulders. "What happened here," he wondered, "what went wrong?"

As he stepped in closer to the chaos, he took a second look at a familiar shape. Jacob saw Clint Borgam, his boss, and he could feel his stomach shrink and sink deep down inside of him. It was unusual to see the old grump at any project site, especially this late in the evening. To top it off, the man never went anywhere without wearing his gear. Tonight, he stood amongst the bloodied scene in tennis shoes, and an orange and green hoodie with blue jeans. Jacob wondered why he noticed his tennis shoes. "Must've been in a hurry to get here. Great, he'll be in a ripe mood, I'm sure," he thought to himself as he looked down at his own appearance. Quickly he tucked the remaining portions of his shirt in, and re-buttoned all but the collar buttons of his shirt, leaving the top undone, and ran his fingers gently through his hair. He shook his hands, and started walking towards Borgam.

Clint, a man in his late sixties, athletic build remnant from his stint as a US Marine, was rubbing the sweat from his forehead while surveying the scene. Jacob knew Clint Borgam had seen it all, and he knew by the look on Clint's face that this situation was dire.

Jacob looked around at the remaining standing men, hoping there was something left of his crew. The team he worked so diligently with through all hours of preparation and training. He was confident in his crew. He knew that nothing could go wrong. They'd perfected every step in the exercise room time and time again.

How could this happen? Where were his men?

Meanwhile, the Lable'ist truck had stopped and the driver was now out walking on foot into the brush of the mountainside. The news crew parked their van a short distance away, and hid it behind some bushes as best they could. Steve Maders, with video camera in hand, followed quietly behind the walking man. Rachelle and Joe, not having seen Steve walk off, were placing the last branch of leaves by the van's tires.

Suddenly, they heard a familiar man's voice yell out, "No!" and then a round of gunshots, obvious gunshots, and they ducked down quickly behind the van.

"Oh-god, where's Steve?" Joe whispered in Rachelle's direction. She looked at him, and seeing fright written across his face, a fright she, too, felt equally, answered, "I don't know."

"Come on, Rach, we got to get out of here!"

She grabbed his arm, "Shh!"

Footsteps. They heard someone getting closer, but the person was obviously approaching slowly, with caution, as would a man in hunt mode, trying to silence his footsteps across the sticks and dry leaves as to not scare away his prey. Sweat was pouring from Joe's forehead, and he was shivering violently. Rachelle looked down at the leaves and dirt ground below them as she felt a warm liquid swallow around her feet. She looked at Joe, disgusted, "Damn it, Joe, you just pissed your freaking pants! You got it all over me!"

Another gunshot. This time, they could hear it was aimed into the air, not like the others. Rachelle grabbed Joe's arm and pulled him her direction, and they quickly climbed into the van from the rear doors. Rachelle squirmed to the front seat as quickly as possible, started the engine, shoved it into reverse, and pressed her foot to the gas pedal. Looking behind her to see where she was driving, she did not notice the short man only feet in front of their van. Jerking her head forward as she ducked down in her seat, she could see this short man now, his silhouette powerful, as he shot off another round, piercing bullets through their windshield; one hitting the driver's side mirror, and one squarely through Joe's shoulder. Joe immediately passed out, the fear too great for him.

Rachelle raced down the hill towards town to the Interstate. She reached I5, swerved impractically through traffic, driving on the shoulder when she had to, and on down the road as fast as she could make that old van go. She finally felt a hand reach out and touch her leg. "Joe!"

"Ya' . . . what happened?" Eyes rolling slowly, out of focus, he looked over his bloodied shoulder towards the back of the van, and asked, "Where's Steve?"

"You've been shot, man. Holy shit, that was intense! I think . . . I think that man shot him, Joe. Ooh-man . . . what . . . what hospital should I take you to?" Rachelle rambled out nervously.

Joe shook his head slightly, "I don't know." He was feeling faint still, and seeing the blood gushing over his fingers as he held pressure on the wound, he did just that after answering, "Probably by my house . . . go downtown."

"That's another thirty minutes away, Joe, shit!" And Rachelle gassed it.

Back at the project site, Jacob picked up his pace, too, and hurried towards Borg am, reporting his arrival. Jacob inquired, "What's the status of the situation here, Sir?"

Clint Borgam was irate! "Who the hell do you think you are, Willem, rushing in here like you own the place? If you were truly in charge, I sure as shit wouldn't be standing here staring at your ugly mug. So why don't YOU tell ME what in god's green earth is going on here, Boy! What's the status of your men?" he yelled at Jacob.

Jacob was dumbfounded. For the first time in his life, he didn't have the answers. He didn't know how to fix this and to make it better. He was speechless.

CHAPTER 7

CRIONE AGENCY

Memories flooded Jacob's mind from the time he had just graduated with honors from *Massachusetts Institute of Technology, in Cambridge, MA. He was a brilliant young Nuclear Engineer Specialist, and minored in Architecture. The government, among many other agencies, had all been eyeing Jacob's work through-out his career at *MIT. Frank Calister, always a man to follow orders, had perfected persistence. He was the President of Crione Agency, the Criminal Response agency for Interrogation and Nuclear Engineering. Calister was impressed with Jacob Willem and followed his every move. He promised Jacob a future, money, stability, creative freedom, and power. When it came down to crunch time, Jacob accepted the job near the Glacier Point Peak Pass facility with the Crione Agency.

Calister had flown Jacob to the project site the prior year. Crione associates briefed him on the minor details of the location. In the beginning, all he'd known of the location was that it was an abandoned water shed left over from the 1940's nuclear program, and it was near some mountain called, Glacier Point Peak Pass. He knew that it was somewhere in Washington on the West Coast.

Jacob was blind folded for unexplained "precautionary reasons" during the end of the helicopter flight when they were approaching the mountain. Jacob was young, newly married, and impressed with Calister. He figured if they were going to invest so much into him, they had to have his best interest in mind. He was also naive.

The mountain was hollow and all that was left of it was the exoskeleton covered in rich green trees. Jacob was told he would be in charge of designing and building holding tanks for weapons, and training crews how to properly handle said weapons.

Being from the plains in Irvine, TX and high school in Omaha, NE, Jacob was taken aback by the enormity and grandiose of the mountains. It was a new and ideal place for him to put his talents to work, he thought. He was young, excited, full of ambition, and allotted a project budget with no limit. All he knew is that he would be briefed on the details when he arrived on site. Later he learned that was near Darrington, Washington.

Darrington was a small town full of wood mills and loggers, with a *population of approximately 1300 people, all of whom seemed to be accustomed to their rituals of grocery shopping on Thursdays, booze at the only local pub on Saturday night, late evening hang out spots at the only bus stop in town, and of course, church on Sunday at any of the given dozen denominations.

After he and Naomi moved there, they purchased their property just outside of Darrington in a town the locals called Whitehorse. Though it was only six miles out from Darrington, it was more dense in the mountains, had a *population of only 180 people, and sat right on the river at the foot of Glacier Point Peak. It was absolutely beautiful there. They would be surrounded by all of Mother Nature's elements. The people were friendly, yet minded their own business, a quality of living that the young Willems easily adapted to.

Jacob and Naomi grew very fond of their new home, and their new surroundings, quickly. Naomi often wondered about her once was best friend that had moved near there, too, in Ballard, for a nursing job years ago. That was only about an hour away. Jacob thought back, remembering it had all seemed so perfect a plan.

Clint Borgam was standing over Jacob who quickly realized he had completely blacked out. Clint's mouth was moving, but Jacob could not hear him. His yelling shot spit onto Jacob's face as he shook his shoulders, "Wake up, Willem, snap out of it!"

When Jacob came to, he stood to face Clint; his hand still rested on Clint's shoulder for balance, and asked what had happened.

"You fell, Boy. Flat on your ass. No way to treat a superior officer." Clint's tone cracked, and a grim grin escaped his expressionless face, then immediately back to his stern approach of things, continued, "You're okay, now suck it up, man. I need the briefings from your exercises. Who was the chink in your chain, so to speak?"

Jacob was afraid to answer that. Not only did he despise Clint's racially biased lingo, he was afraid this so called chink in the chain, would be himself. He had to find out what had happened.

"Borgam, I need a little time to debrief my crew. Do you know if any of my men are left alive in there? Have you briefed Calister?"

"No, but you have 'til five minutes ago to find out and report your status back to me. I'll handle Calister."

"Yes, Sir." Jacob turned, walking towards the opening at the crevasse of the mountainside that would lead him to the tunnel.

He shook his head, feeling astonished at the situation he was in. How did he ever let this happen? How did he end up testing protective shells to hold bio terrorist bombs inside of a mountain? How did he ever become the Head Engineer for the Crione Agency's nuclear program anyway? What qualifications did a once-a-college-student have to risk life and limb of the people who worked for him and trusted him so blindly? How had Frank Calister known the details of his life, and his father's work history? What made him justify a lie to Naomi all these years about his profession as a nuclear scientist and head engineer? That's why he couldn't have a conversation with her about his days at work. He couldn't stand to lie to her anymore. He could justify being silent.

"Damn it," he cried out in frustration and the anger he'd suppressed for so many years. Pushing his way through the smoke filled opening, he couldn't imagine what he was about to uncover after the mess of debris and scattered bloodshed outside that he had already walked through. His head was aching. He felt faint; ears ringing and his veins tingled with pain. Every bone in his body seemed to be encased in poison. What the hell was going on with his body? He couldn't focus like this.

Down the corridor of the mountainside entryway, plastic tarps were wrapped around body shaped figures like mummies. He counted ten, and stopped, allowing his eyes to gloss over as he took in the blur of bodies. There were crews putting out remaining fires, men running with equipment on their backs in and out of the tunnel, and other men loading these tarps of body shapes into large trucks. People were yelling, though there seemed to be an eerie silence among the crew leaders standing in circles talking amongst themselves.

As Jacob Willem passed by a group of people and workers, they silenced their words, and stared at him blankly. Jacob heard a voice call out to ask where he had been as the voice of Tommy Krindle approached him; Jacob's emotions felt numb, angry. He had always wondered exactly what role Tommy played at Crione, but respected the confidentiality of their roles, and never pressed him about it. Tommy was much older than Jacob, a short man, the thin and fit, cyclist type of guy. When Tommy was around, there was always a party after work, usually at any local bar they could come across. A few times, they'd gone down to Seattle and took Tommy's boathouse out. Tommy always had a different girl with him, so much younger than he, and it seemed the man was never sober. Jacob had never seen Tommy at the office either, and seldom would be briefed by him at the project site on new techniques Jacob was being ordered to put into practice.

Tommy told Jacob that all of his crew was trapped inside the tunnel. He tried to explain that there was an explosion in the holding tanks, and that they had no way to get to his men. "When the explosion went off, the tanks shot out large pieces of metal in every direction. It was like a thousand shotguns went off at the same time. The welding gave out, and the tanks collapsed, setting off some of the weapons inside. Fortunately most of the leakage was contained. We both know this could have been much worse. Part of the tunnel collapsed. Most of the rocks and dirt are on top of the crew. There was blood everywhere, man. Where have you been anyway? We couldn't get to them, Willem, all of them. They're all trapped in there. I'm sorry." Jacob didn't respond to a word Tommy told him, barely looked the man in the eye as he spoke. Jacob felt suddenly unattached, and felt his blood grow cold. He patted Tommy on the shoulder, and continued to walk by. The ringing in Jacob's ears turned deafening as he tried to remain focused. Tommy continued speaking, "There's no way to say what exactly has happened to cause all of this, Willem. We'd hoped you would have had this situation under control by now . . . but this one, Willem . . . this one has been a catastrophe. There will be questions to answer to detectives, and the media is already having a frenzy. Be prepared."

Staring straight ahead, Jacob entered the tunnel.

CHAPTER 8

DIDN'T CALL
FOR SMALL TALK

Naomi stood at her bay window, looking outside down their long driveway, and out across the sun scape valley of wild daisies and luscious greenery. The air was moist and heavy, but the cool breeze soothed away the sticky humid kisses. With the phone receiver in her hand held up to her ear, she couldn't believe she had just dialed that number.

"Hello," a woman answered; her voice deep and crisp. Hearing Rose Carson's voice again brought tears immediately to Naomi's eyes. It had been over sixteen years since they had really spoken last.

"Rose. This is Naomi."

Silence. There was an uncomfortable pause, and then Rose cried out questionably, "Naomi?"

Was she excited to hear Naomi's voice? The last time they spoke Naomi threatened to have Rose's nursing license taken away from her, and threatened to "take it to every news station in the US!" Naomi could hear her own words from many years ago. So dramatic. She felt so guilty all these years for being so mad at her friend just because she decided not to be a surrogate carrier for her. How selfish of her, she thought, after all, that is a huge responsibility and sacrifice. In that moment, Naomi was flooded with the pain and hurt she felt only a few years after that. How had that not taken precedence over the other thought, she couldn't make sense of. Her thoughts and their silence was interrupted with Rose's voice.

"Naomi? Are you there? I . . . I wouldn't have thought in a million years to ever hear from you again! How are you? I miss you." Rose's voice faded to a deep whisper.

"I didn't call for the small talk, Rose. Is Jacob with you?"

"Heavens no, Naomi! Why on earth would you ask me that?"

They talked for nearly two hours. Naomi told her about the night before when Jacob left so quickly. She told her about the explosions. They talked about how sick he'd been for the last several months. Naomi didn't dare discuss their sex life with Rose, though. That was none of her damn business, she thought to herself. She talked about her painting again, and the gallery event coming up in three weeks. "Maybe you could come," Naomi could not believe she invited her. Rose used to be her dearest friend after all, she justified to herself. She could forgive, but she could never forget. Naomi's mothers' words rang clear in her head.

"A lot of water under our bridge, my friend. Are you sure you would want me there?" Rose asked.

"Yes. Please come." Naomi hung up the phone, and sat back in her comfy chair, curling her legs beneath her.

She called Jacob's cell again. Still no answer.

CHAPTER 9

911

The drive home seemed to take an eternity. Jacob's mind was swirling with all that had transpired in the past hours since he left the house yesterday. He couldn't focus, and so he pulled off to the side of the road. Placing his face in his hands, he rubbed his palms up and down quickly several times, trying to snap himself out of it, or back into it. Whatever "it" was. He needed sleep. He felt so nauseous, so dizzy.

He turned the radio on, and slipped the Bob Dylan CD in the disk player. Dylan always soothed Jacob. He loved his music. The irony of Dylan's voice grounded him. Bob Dylan's voice whined, * "The answer is blowing in the wind, the answer, my friend, is blowing in the wind."

Jacob's mind drifted back to Rose Carson. Why was he thinking of her? He had so many regrets. That was so long ago. He thought about her almost every day, thought about calling her. He felt like he needed to apologize to her for some reason, or to yell at her and blame her for everything wrong in his life. He didn't know, and he would never call anyway. Not after how Naomi reacted after he told her what was going on back in Cambridge his junior year. He did it for her anyway. At least that's what he had told himself in the beginning.

Memories flashed of him holding Naomi's hand at the E.R. after she lost the baby. It was nineteen years ago, but only months into their marriage. Jacob was on spring break, and they'd gone to Nebraska to visit his family. Rose Carson, who had moved back to Cambridge from Washington after hearing of Naomi's pregnancy, had come along with them back to Omaha, but she had gone off to visit some old friends and her cousins. Jacob and Naomi were having dinner at his parents' house.

31

His mother, Florence Willem, was an exquisite cook. She had made them a Tuscan meal of finely cut slices of steak sautéed in a succulent sauce only Jacob's mother knew the recipe for, homemade sourdough bread, and a salad to die for; fresh greens, spinach leaves, Kalamata olives, feta cheese, thinly sliced red onion, cherry tomatoes, lightly peppered, and tossed with a balsamic vinegar and olive oil.

His father, Richard Willem, poured glasses of a sweet Riesling wine and sparkling water for Naomi. They all stood and held hands as Richard gave thanks in prayer for their family and meal. He asked for blessings on their family as his son, Jacob, and his daughter in law, Naomi, started their own family. Not a moment had passed after Richard said, "Amen," when Naomi collapsed to the floor. Blood and fluids sprawled out from between her legs. She grabbed at her stomach, curled in a ball as she lay on their thick carpeted floor, sobbing from pain. She was speaking, but Jacob could not understand her. He was frozen still. Terrified and motionless.

She was four months along, hardly showing, but had horrible pains the entire time. Naomi knew the moment she became pregnant. She had that instinctual intuition about her. She always "just knew."

Jacob's father rushed them to the hospital after Jacob carried his new wife and soon to be child growing inside of her, to Florence's mini-van. Even though Richard was speeding, and running red lights, the drive seemed like it took a decade. "Hurry, Dad! Oh-God, please . . . hurry!" Jacob pleaded in a desperate cry.

Richard pulled up to the emergency entrance at the hospital moments later, and Jacob was out the door before they were parked. He opened Naomi's car door and swooped her into his arms. She hugged his body as he hurried into the hospital yelling for help, "Please, someone help us!" Their blood soaked clothes tore slowly away from each other as nurses rushed Naomi away, not allowing Jacob to follow along.

He never understood why, but that sound . . . the sound of their clothes pulling away as the nurses took her from his arms. He'd never forgotten that sound. Often, it woke him from his sleep.

"I'm so tired," he said aloud as he realized he was drifting into oncoming traffic. Swerving to avoid a dog running across the road, he gained his composure, and focused on staying between the lines on his side of the road this time. His eyes began to blur, and the ringing in his ears; piercing.

His thoughts drifted again, to when he sat with his father, Richard, in the waiting room. The doctor came out to talk with them; Jacob felt everything go numb inside of him. Afterward, he couldn't remember much of the doctor's words. As the doctor walked away, all Jacob knew was that Naomi had a miscarriage, and that they had to perform an emergency hysterectomy. "There's no baby, Mr. Willem. Naomi will never have children." Those were the only words he could remember hearing. The doctor's voice. Over and over again in his head. "Naomi will never have children. There's no baby . . ."

"I'm so sorry, Son," said Richard, catching Jacob as he felt his body fall limp against his father.

Rose Carson had been Naomi's best friend for as long as they could remember. She was a nurse, and Naomi's mid-wife. Richard beeped Rose's pager number, "9-1-1." Rose knew what to do and headed for the hospital.

When she arrived, the worst had already been done. All she could do now was console her friends, Naomi and Jacob.

Chapter 10

Cambridge

After losing the baby, Jacob, Naomi, and Rose returned to Cambridge. Jacob continued his studies at MIT, and Rose stayed at her cheap apartment she'd moved into not far away from theirs. Naomi seemed to be oblivious to her surrounding reality; her art became dark and smeared. Over the course of those months following her miscarriage, she fell into a deep depression. She stopped painting, stopped eating, and stopped talking. Hell, she might as well have stopped breathing. When the doctors told her they had to perform an emergency . . . she couldn't even think of that word, much less speak it. Hysterectomy . . . she could never have children. She could never feel her baby grow inside of her. She could never be a mother. She was exhausted and feeling a despair never felt before.

Times were stress filled then for her and Jacob. They hardly spoke, and when they did, they would fight. Not about anything specific. Just fight. That's all they knew how to do anymore, it seemed. It was easier than pretending to be okay or pretending to be happy any longer. Their "best summer of all times" was definitely over.

After losing a baby, and hopes for a family, what did they have to fight for anymore, Jacob often wondered? However, he never once thought of leaving her. Fighting is what they became good at, until it too stopped, and silence took over their home.

Rose would stop by almost daily to check on them. She always said she was checking in on Naomi, but she cared about Jacob also. Heck, she thought, he lost a baby, too. She wanted to slap her friend at times, and give her a wakeup call. Naomi was so depressed, she wasn't herself anymore. The experience had awaken a bitterness and selfishness inside of Naomi, a self-righteous owning of resentment.

One day Rose carried in a handful of magazines, brochures, and manuals when she came to visit Naomi. She left them on Naomi's bedside table without a mention.

Later that night, Naomi noticed the awkward stack of papers and magazines, and picked the top one up to read it. It was a manual on group counseling for women who had lost a child. Naomi threw the manual across the room, its thick pages hurling through the air and colliding against the bedroom closet doors, then sliding down to the carpet floor. "I didn't lose a child, mine was taken from me!" she cried aloud. She picked up the next one. It read something about miscarriages. The next one was a magazine. The cover displayed two women, one pregnant, and a man. The title read, "The Surrogate Way." Naomi opened to the center of the magazine to read the article, and there was a sticky-note from Rose. She wrote, "Call me."

When Rose answered the phone, Naomi didn't give her a chance to say hello.

"Would you really be willing to do that for me, Rose?" The silence comforted Naomi. She suddenly didn't care about not being able to have her own child grow inside of her. Her uterus was taken from her, but she no longer cared that their child wouldn't be her own. The sensation feeling a life develop within her and birthed from her own body was not as important as the ideals ahead of them now. She longed so badly for the family that she and Jacob had talked endless hours about. She longed to mother his child. She longed for their family to become so, to be blessed with the honor and responsibilities of molding a young mind, to give it the love and devotion only a real parent could offer, both a mother and a father, unlike anything she had ever known in her childhood. She knew what was truly important now, and felt elated inside that her best friend would do something so selfless for her.

Rose answered softly, "Of course. Anything for you guys. I would be honored."

Three weeks later, the doctor visit for Rose went well. The news about the artificial insemination financial requirements, however were not that welcoming; more sad news. She couldn't tell Naomi. She knew Naomi and Jacob could not afford it right now. Instead Rose called Jacob, and they met at a local park near MIT. Rose asked Jacob not to tell Naomi about any of this, but that she had a plan. Rose explained she had to return to

Washington, catch up on schooling, but gave him her mobile number, and address on 9th Street in Ballard, WA. She told him to expect a call from her, and that he would need to fly out alone if he decided to take her up on her offer.

Naomi and Jacob were still not communicating well, and she worried constantly why she hadn't heard back from her dear friend, Rose. Naomi had left Rose numerous voice mails, went to her apartment, called her mobile phone, and her dad's place. Rose continually avoided her. Excuse after excuse, Rose finally told Naomi she hadn't gone to the doctor yet for her follow up. Eventually they had gotten into an argument about Rose breaking her promise to Naomi. Rose told her she was sorry but she had changed her mind, and that she needed to go back to school. "Now just isn't the right time," she told her friend. Naomi was crushed, feeling helpless, and responded out of desperation, anger, and disappointment.

Over the course of the years that Jacob attended MIT, Rose hadn't spoken to her friend, Naomi, or to Jacob, until a few weeks before his junior year came to an end in 1991. Rose secretly called Jacob to come and visit her in Washington. He agreed to meet her in one month at a local pub on 9th Street downtown near Rose's apartment complex in Ballard, WA, called St. Patrick's Den. After learning that Crione Agency would be flying him to Washington, even though he didn't really know exactly where in Washington he would be taken to, he thought that none of that mattered. This was his opportunity. To him, there was no other choice. He had to meet with Rose. He had to do this for Naomi, he told himself, for their marriage, for the family they wanted so badly, and selfishly for the wife and friend in Naomi he had missed so badly since she lost their baby. Somehow, this all made sense to him. He knew he had to go through with it, besides, Rose wasn't exactly hard on the eyes anyway, he thought.

Jacob was nervous. He arrived at the pub an hour and a half earlier than they intended on meeting. When Rose walked in and sat next to him, she could smell the alcohol on his breath. She thought that was a great idea. "I'll have the same as this guy," she said to the bartender as she motioned to her friend, Jacob. "And make it a double."

Several months later, the phone at Naomi and Jacob's house rang. It was Rose. Naomi was shocked to hear from her friend. She tried to tell her that she came out to WA to make amends with her a couple years ago. Rose interrupted her to say, "Naomi, I have to tell you something . . ."

Sobbing, Naomi hung up the phone. Rose also had lost Jacob's baby . . . that Naomi had known nothing about.

Naomi marched to her and Jacobs's bedroom, where they had shared so many sweet and private moments together. She gathered all of his clothes from his closet. She hugged them close to her, smelling his scent on everything she touched. She stood, frozen still, sobbing, "How could she . . . how could they . . ." she wondered aloud. Anger replaced tears, and she proceeded to gather the rest of Jacob's belongings from the bathroom, and dresser drawers. She emptied the contents of his desk drawers into a box, and called her mother, Irene O'Brien, who always moved within a few miles of them every time they moved. Irene was the type of mother who was waiting for her child to return back home, waiting for the bad and the ugly so she could come to the rescue and be the hero.

When Jacob came home that day, all of his belongings laid burned on the front lawn, with a picket sign perched beside the lump of waste, stating "Cheaters will be shot. Betrayal kills." Naomi's mother was there by her side through the entire episode, every step, and crumpled newspaper. She provided the lighter fluid, and had handed Naomi the match.

Jacob was devastated. He couldn't bear tell Naomi about secretly meeting Rose all those months ago, and he sure as hell hadn't heard from Rose since. It took months of attempting to talk with Naomi about what happened. Finally he wrote her a letter, professing his love for her, confessing his hurt, his loneliness, his mourning of their longed for family. He was drunk, it was Rose's idea, and he swore they slept together only that one time. He begged Naomi for forgiveness, and asked for her compassion to reach out to him. He needed his best friend, his love, his joy. He wrote that he did this all for them, for the family that they talked about, and when Rose called him nearly three years ago and offered to carry their child again, he felt as though it was their last and only chance; the only choice, provided their lack of income at the time. He knew he would never be able to financially afford the artificial insemination procedure they had once looked into. He knew now that all of this was wrong. He couldn't bear hurting her and that was why he had kept it a secret. He wrote that he loved her, and only her. He asked that she find it in her heart to forgive him, to trust him that he would never make such a mistake again, never had since then, and he would never make a decision without her again . . . he would do anything she could ever request of him, just to make it up to her.

Naomi's mother was against forgiving any man, telling Naomi she might forgive, but she will never forget. "How could you ever forget that?" Irene would ask matter of factly as though there were never reason behind action, whether it is right or wrong. After Naomi found out that her mother had lied about hiding the fact that Jacob had been calling the house to talk with her, she told her mom that she had crossed a line, and it wasn't her right to keep her from talking to her husband. Several weeks went by when Naomi heard the news of Jacob's sister having died in a horrible car accident back in Omaha. She called Jacob and agreed to meet him at his hotel room where he had been staying since she kicked him out. They cried, and talked until dawn. Watching the sunrise together, Jacob took Naomi in his arms, and promised to never hurt her again.

Naomi decided to forgive him. Jacob moved back in the house. They never spoke of those times again, and Naomi never spoke to Rose again. Her mother stopped coming by the house, and soon their seldom phones calls even stopped. Nearly an entire year passed before Naomi began to paint again, and then it was time for the big move. Washington bound.

Chapter 11

Bad Day

Jacob swung their heavy custom made redwood front door wide open and stepped inside. It was late in the afternoon.

"Bad day?" Naomi called out from the back of the house. She hadn't asked him how his day was in years. Was she being sarcastic, he wondered. Her tone was cynical, mad maybe. He knew he looked awful, bags under eyes, smelling of dirt, dried blood, and his clothes smoke stained from the explosion. Ignoring her remark, he headed straight for the shower.

Naomi barged into the bathroom. His dirty clothes laid across the towel rack. They wreaked something fierce. Was that blood on his cheek? She demanded to know who was on the phone before he left last night. Jacob didn't answer. He was exhausted. He didn't want to argue. "Where were you all night?" she asked, her voice dry and monotone.

"I told you, I was at the office."

"Why didn't you answer my calls then?"

"Hey, you know my cell doesn't get good reception inside that building. I'm sorry, my joy. Really, I am. I'm so tired. Let me take a shower and I'll come and sit with you for dinner." Jacob wouldn't look her in the eye, he was too tired anyway. He wondered if she suspected anything of him. "How couldn't she?" he wondered to himself, hoping to God she wouldn't notice his dirty clothes beside her.

Never really having gotten over his betrayal so many years ago, Naomi's anger reverted to suspicion. "Dinner? Are you delusional? Don't you realize it's the middle of afternoon, the next day? You must think I'm an idiot . . . if you think for one minute that I'm going to put up with you cheating on me, you can forget it!" Naomi snapped. "You and your mistress can

39

have each other for all I care!" She turned and saw that his clothes were incredibly dirtied. "At the office, aye?"

Calmly Jacob replied, as heartfelt as he could muster through his exhaustion, "Don't be ridiculous, Naomi, my true treasure is wherever my heart is . . . and my heart is yours. Tell me you know that!"

"Go to hell!" She slammed the bathroom door, and stormed out of the house. She needed to blow off steam. She surrendered to the riverside, walking briskly, until she realized she had been holding her breath for what felt like a mile. She took a deep breath in, slowly exhaling, slowed to a comfortable mosey, picked up a few flat pebbles and then skipped them across the glistening water. After at least an hour's passing, she thought about their argument and those words that spewed from her mouth. She hadn't even give him a chance to wind-down, much less to explain, she told herself. Deciding she would head back home, and apologize for over reacting, she picked up the pace and headed back the direction she had come. Still, she thought, "I need to demand an explanation."

Thoughts drifting away from her, "Why did you call Rose?" she asked aloud to herself. Sigh.

She remembered Jacob hadn't answered her emails either. Yes, that would be her next question. "Jacob, if you were at the office all night and day, why didn't you respond to my email?"

CHAPTER 12

TOO FAR

Jacob stepped out of the shower, his stomach aching so badly, he felt like someone had poisoned him. Feeling faint, he lost his balance and stumbled towards the floor, catching himself with one hand on the wall while hugging his stomach with his other forearm. "I feel like I'm going to throw up," he said to himself. Then hurling himself in the direction of the toilet, he caught himself with each hand opposite the other, on the sides of the porcelain bowl. The pain spread to his sides, and up his back, then into his head. He felt its every movement, as though this poison inside of him was a living thing wearing cleats as it crawled through his veins and along his skin.

"Naomi!" He called out. No response. She was too far away, and could not hear him.

He wiped his mouth with tissue paper, and crawled to the sink where he pulled himself up to his feet. Rinsing his mouth, he spit out the watered down acidic fluid, while placing both hands on the marble counter to ground himself. So cold, he thought. He tried to focus on his reflection in the mirror. He reached out his hand and placed his palm on the glass, smeared in one long heavy swoop to clear the mist, and realized he could not focus. His eyes were a blur. Feeling dizzy still, he thought aloud, "Maybe I need to lie down."

Stumbling to the bed while holding his stomach, he laid on his side, legs and feet still hanging off the edge; no strength to pull them up onto the bed. He let his body fall onto its back, staring above; the ceiling began to circle. "Ugh-I have to sit up," he mumbled out loud. Propping himself up, he realized he was going to have to go to the hospital again. "Naomi," he desperately yelled out. Still, there was no answer.

41

Rising from his bed, Jacob dressed himself slowly, grabbed his keys and headed outside, down the long driveway to his truck.

Down the road a ways, it had started to rain, and he could barely see in front of him. Was it the rain or his eyes, he wondered. Cranking the defroster to high, and turning on the windshield wipers, he reached for his cell phone to call Naomi. Patting to feel around at the passenger seat with his right hand, he tried to keep his eyes on the road. "Damn it." He'd forgotten his mobile. "I'll call from the E.R.," he said aloud.

He longed for Naomi and wished he could tell her about his work. Would she forgive me again? Would she understand? Would she leave me? He wondered to himself. His mind wandered to Rose, and Borgam, and Calister. "What a mess," he said.

Suddenly feeling faint again, he began to swerve. All of the lights were going dim around him. He couldn't keep his eyes open. His body aching, he said aloud, "I'm so tired." Darkness engulfed his surroundings. He'd gone unconscious.

From the opposite direction was an approaching van; they'd just left the emergency room downtown. Swerving to avoid hitting the big truck head on that they saw coming at them full speed the wrong direction, they came to a screeching halt in the dirt aside the road. The driver of the van yelled out, "Shit!" Her heart racing, not realizing she was holding her breath, and that her fists were gripping the steering wheel so tight that her knuckles had turned white, she looked back towards the inside of the van frantically. All the equipment seemed to stay in place, a few loose binders and notepads; she glanced over at her passenger. He was knocked unconscious. Shaking her passenger gently, "Joe, are you okay? Joe!" He woke to see his co-worker, Rachelle Wong, calling out to him, a frantic look on her face. This made him laugh. Pushing her hand away, "I'm fine, you sap. Look at you!" Laughing still. "You're delirious," Joe Stanley retorted.

Rachelle responded, half embarrassed, "Hey, let's just go. We're gonna miss all the noise at the office about last night, and we've gotta figure out what to do about Steve."

That very moment, they both heard loud screeching of tires, and the sound of swerving cars only disturbed traffic makes. Looking in their side view mirrors, they saw a big truck toppling over and over again, sparks flying all about, until finally the mass of metal circling through the air came to a stop in the ditch beside the dirt where they, too, had stopped only yards away. "Grab the camera," Rachelle yelled to Joe as she hopped out the driver's door and ran towards the crash site. Glass was everywhere; a tire wheel had broken off and lay in the middle of the street. There were "rubberneckers" slowing down to see exactly what had happened, and a few witnesses standing on sidewalks watching in horror and amazement, gawking and pointing. All that was missing was the popcorn! A man came running across the street towards the site, nearly getting himself hit by an oncoming vehicle. "Stop there," Rachelle yelled out.

She reached the truck finally. It was lying upside down, doors crushed nearly flat, scraps of metal flung in every direction, and no reminisce of the once was window panels. She yelled towards the truck, "Hello, are you okay?" There, of course, was no answer, and she waved at Joe to stop rolling. "Call 911. I think this one's a goner."

Suddenly there was a deafening sound from a semi-truck's screeching tires and brakes, trying to come to a quick stop. Rachelle turned her head, looking behind over her shoulder, as she was still knelt down by the mass of crumpled metal that Jacob Willem lay trapped in, time seemed to speed in fast forward mode. She watched helplessly as the semi-truck collided against her co-worker's body. Flesh, blood, and bits of body parts flung in every direction, as she reached her arm out straight towards him, and she screamed, "No!"

CHAPTER 13

NOT JUST AN ENGINEER

Rachelle Wong's nerves were shot. Sitting in the middle of wreckage, she looked around at the sight, and felt sick to her stomach. Her mind began reeling over everything that had happened, faster than she could make sense of. She was scared and devastated for the loss of her news team. Her sound guy and close friend, Joe, had just been annihilated in front of her own eyes by an out of control semi-truck driver, and her cameraman, Steve, was now missing. Who was that short man on the mountain? What was he protecting? Why was he shooting at them?

She waited as calmly as she could for the ambulance to arrive at the scene of the accident. Looking around, she could not believe there were no people left standing around. No one was there to help her make sense of any of this. It seemed the only so called witness left was the truck driver who just killed her sound man. "Where is everyone? Where's the police?" Rachelle yelled out! She saw the truck driver on his mobile phone, as he was running towards her. Rachelle noticed her hands, not only were they shaking, but her entire body felt out of control. Was she having a heart attack? "Is this what a mental breakdown feels like?" she asked herself aloud.

It felt like hours later, but the police finally arrived. She gave her statements to the young police officer who was first on the scene. She didn't tell him anything about being on that mountain, or about how she and Joe left Steve there because of the gun shots. She did not tell him that Steve wasn't only missing; but that she was certain he had just been murdered.

The paramedics looked her over, advised she allow them to take her to the ER, or have a police officer escort her home, but she insisted she was fine and did not need any assistance. She told them all that she was just in shock, very tired, but that she would be fine, and that she was due back at the news station hours ago. After having been given permission by the police officer to leave, Rachelle returned to her van.

Not certain of where she would go now, and feeling a sudden flood of anxiety about calling the station right now, she told herself, "that would have to wait". Bob Milson was already irate that they hadn't gotten any footage of the mountain the day before, and seemed heartless about the news of Steve missing. He said he would handle calling in the missing person report, but that Rachelle and Joe were to stay with the story. "You're right, Joe, he is a prick," she said silently to her now deceased sound man. Deciding then she couldn't bare talking to her supervisor, Bob, that moment; she opened her Blackberry and sent an email to him instead. Rachelle told him there had been an accident, and Joe was hit and killed by a semi-truck. She asked what the police told him about Steve being missing, and told him she was going to go home now, and that she needed a few days off. She told him she already talked to the police about witnessing the truck accident, and the semi that hit Joe. She ended by adding that if Bob had any questions, to call her tomorrow.

Simultaneously, the paramedics were tending to Jacob's crash and the semi-truck accident with victim, Joe Stanley. EMTs soon realized that they would not be able extract Jacob from his truck without a mechanical force. Trying to get any sort of response from him, an EMT heard a moaning sound come out from within the wreckage and called back to his crew members, "I have a nonsensical response from the victim, male. We'll need the Jaws of Life here."

"Hang on there, Buddy; we're gonna get you out of there! Just stay with me." The EMT called out towards Jacob's demolished truck.

Jacob could hear him this time, still not able to muster any solid words; he continued mumbling whatever sounds he could manage.

After the emergency fire response team extracted Jacob from his rumbled mess of a truck, with the assistance of the Jaws of Life, they quickly realized they were not going to get a logical response from him. He was responsive, but nonsensical. An EMT was searching the debris of the truck, searching for any form of identity. Not on the ground, nor in the truck, nor on his body, could they find a wallet or a cellular phone.

As the remaining EMT crew loaded him onto the stretcher, one asked, "Who do we have here, any name?"

"John Doe. Nonsensical verbal response. Approximately 40 years of age, male, 6'4", vehicle totaled, severe injuries," reported the EMT tending to Jacob.

"Hey, has anyone checked for insurance docs?" another EMT called out.

"Can't get to it."

They loaded him into the back of the ambulance, shut the doors, ignited the sirens, and fled down the crowded city streets. Jacob had fluids oozing from his ears and pores, a thick greenish black unrecognizable fluid. He had a high fever, chills, eyes rolling backward, violent shakes; the thick fluids were beginning to ooze also from his mouth. The EMTs were having a difficult time keeping him stabilized before he eventually went unconscious. "It's almost like he's radioactive, look at his veins, and his skin, it's glowing," an EMT said to another. "Wonder who this guy is."

Arriving at St. Jude's Hospital in downtown Seattle, outside of Ballard, they rushed their said John Doe through the emergency room doors.

Meanwhile, Naomi was walking back home from the river, feeling guilty. She shouldn't have said those things. She only wished Jacob would open up to her, let her in on what was going on around their suddenly chaotic filled lives. Why had they fought? They hardly ever fought, at least not in many years. "Why doesn't he talk to me about his work anymore," she wondered. Why all the secrecy? What are all those explosions in the mountains about? What exactly does he do for Crione Agency anyway? He's just an engineer, right? "All these late hours just don't make any sense," she thought aloud, "and the emergency call?" None of this is adding up, she thought to herself. "My love, what has changed?" she asked at the passing by river's rapids.

They hadn't fought over his work in nearly three years. She was so tired that she couldn't sleep at nights, thoughts of her gallery shows and all the bills to be paid still, she worried now mostly about Jacob, so she turned her Walkman radio volume up to distract herself from her own thoughts. Walking up their driveway, she felt some reprieve from her emotions, and suddenly excited to have a real conversation with her husband, something they hadn't done in a long time. They had mastered the art of small talk within their contentment of marriage. Intellectual conversations, debates on politics and religions, and flirtatious banter became their accustomed dinner table mannerisms with one another. They discussed everything non-personal, unless it involved Naomi's gallery events. She loved to share those details with Jacob, and he enjoyed every moment of the realness behind those conversations.

Plucking off the stem one of Jacob's precious roses and taking in the musky scent through a deep inhale, she entered their house, calling out for Jacob. She realized quickly he wasn't home any longer. "Was the truck outside?" she asked herself. She walked over to the front door window and looked out down the driveway. His truck was gone. "He's mad," she figured. "Must've gone back to work."

Naomi started cleaning the house to occupy her mind. In the den, dusting Jacob's bookshelves, and desk, she noticed the voice mail light flashing. She picked up the cordless phone, pressing the down arrow; she saw a missed call at 10:22pm. from the night before. She listened to the voice mail and realized now exactly how bad she felt. Jacob had called while she was out getting Chinese take out for dinner last night. Still, she wondered, while hanging up the receiver to its charging bay, why the secrecy, and what about my email? He hadn't answered either. She called his cell again, and this time, heard the ringing sing out from their bedroom. "Oh-great," she said, he left it at home. "Must really be upset with me . . ." she confessed to the air.

Another explosion rippled through the air and sent vibrations throughout the house, so fierce this time Naomi lost her balance, and fell to the floor. Scared and frustrated, she whispered, "Damn it . . . definitely a bad day."

CHAPTER 14

ANOTHER EXPLOSION

Clint Borgam had returned to the Glacier Point Peak project site at the Pass. The injured people and chaos seemed to be mostly cleared out. There were still a few remaining people walking about, cleaning up the debris from the explosions earlier. Overlooking the scene playing out in front of him, Borgam saw Tommy Krindle exiting the tunnel from the mountain's entrance way. As Borgam approached Krindle, he called out, "Sir. I have orders to brief you on the interior damages from the explosions," and as he passed by, Krindle simply turned to follow him.

Entering the holding tank room for the bio terrorist nuclear weapons stored in safety tanks that Jacob Willem had designed, engineered, and had his team build; large metal boxes with a thick glass front exposing a display of sorts of the interior shells, weaponry, and bio terrorist warheads held inside, Borgam pointed out to Krindle the damage caused from the tank's support beams connected to the scaffolding built against the innards of the mountainside interior walls; mirroring the image of a gigantic metal spider web that had collapsed in exasperating areas from faulty welded joints. When the joints gave out from being weighed down, the scaffolding crumbled in areas, causing large beams to crash down onto the majority of the holding tanks. Scraps of metal pierced some of the warheads, and the friction caused a spark which ignited the place up like bombs had exploded.

"There was nothing we could do," Borgam explained to Krindle. "Some of these warheads have been leaking for years. We just discovered that in recent months, due to the tanks being punctured by the breaking support beams to the interior of the tanks. It wasn't noticeable until one finally ignited and caused the first explosion months ago." Pausing,

Borgam thought carefully about what next to say as Krindle remained silent, all ears. Knowing Krindle's fondness of Jacob Willem, Borgam continued, "We do have Willem to thank for these tanks, Sir. His work has been effective. If these warheads were not properly secured, not accurately contained, these explosions . . . . they would have been more like . . . ." he paused before continuing, "the *Trinity Fireball of 1945. I'm afraid, Sir, there's a lot of . . . cleaning up to do here. If our government and overseas accounts, with their authorities, find out that we were responsible for setting off nuclear warheads . . . Well, I'm sure I don't have to tell you what might happen to this company, much less our reputations and careers."

Tommy Krindle, the quiet tempered, demanding man that he was, finally responded in a firm manner, "Informative, Borgam. Thank you. Let's not speculate as to what will happen to my reputation, career, or with Crione Agency. It was your responsibility to oversee this project and to assure its safety, and top level secrecy, to our clients and crews. You have failed, and you will have to face your own repercussions. Willem had done his job, but with obvious flaws. Flaws that were detected months ago you tell me now! These leaks should have been contained then. Where is Willem now?"

"Yes, Sir, Willem is . . . non-respondent. I have not been able to locate him since he left here. He reportedly was not feeling well, went home to shower and rest. I'd instructed him to report back to me ASAP, but have not heard from him yet, Sir," Borgam replied.

"I don't care what it takes, Borgam, get rid of the rest of these bodies, hide the remaining weapons in the sealed containment room in back, clean up the so called explosion leaks, and seal off the damn tunnel entrance already! Is that clear?" Krindle barked, having lost his patience.

The evening's dusk was approaching quickly. As Borgam was following his orders from Krindle, picking up small pieces of debris to appear busy, he decidedly called out to Krindle, telling Krindle to follow him to the containment room. Begrudgingly, Krindle followed; curious as to what else Borgam had to confess.

They reached the large safe-like, incineration room, nearly empty with exception to another large metal box; this one designed for burning at the highest temperature. Any object thrown into its fiery mouth would be decimated—Borgam slowed his pace and positioned himself steadily in front of Tommy Krindle.

Entering the containment room, Borgam reached in his coat pocket and pulled out a large hunting knife, which he turned with suddenly and stabbed Krindle effectively in the artery of his neck. Borgam caught Krindle as his near lifeless body began to fall, and dragged him to the fiery mouth of the containment box. Pushing Krindle's body squarely into the fiery pit, he shut the door of the containment room behind him, and continued on with his business.

Borgam gathered remaining explosives, which he placed throughout the tunnel as he searched the grounds. Making certain that all was now clear, no covered bodies left exposed outside, and all remaining holding tanks with remaining weapons he also placed inside the containment room. Then he exited the tunnel of the mountain, and ordered the remaining crew members to leave the site.

In his truck, Clint Borgam pressed the button for the detonator, and waited. Moments later, a massive explosion rattled the grounds, and the tunnel was securely sealed shut. His hands firmly gripped to his steering wheel, Borgam's eyes focused sternly out at that mountainside, admiring how his orders had caused their crew to efficiently get the cleanup done. Now, with the realization that Krindle was dead, Borgam felt he would finally get the respect he demanded.

He decided to head home, needing badly to clear his head. He called Frank Calister on the way, and reported the status of the project site, informed him all ties had been severed except that Jacob Willem was non-respondent and . . .

Calister interrupted, "Just handle it," and hung up the receiver.

In the meantime, back at the Willems' house, Naomi called Jacob at the office; four rings, five, six, seven rings . . . no answer. The same with his mobile phone, except it went straight to his voice mail. Feeling worried and anxious, she opened her laptop to send another email, "Please call me," she wrote simply.

Down the hall towards the front door entrance of their home to the den where Jacob would spend sleep lacking nights working from home, was also their house phone. Thinking of the call she watched him answer before rushing out the door, she picked up the receiver and dialed star-6-9 to view the last call received. It was Jacob's mobile number that he called from when he left that voice mail.

Placing the cordless receiver back to its charging station, curiosity set in as to why Jacob had called home from his mobile if he was at his office.

"That's unusual," she said aloud. Scrambling through Jacob's briefcase he had left behind, she searched for answers; answers to what, she was not sure. There were papers from work, outlines for some sort of tank or a box. Confused, she thought to herself, "a large box?" Thumbing through the remaining papers, she found nothing that made real sense to her, nothing that would indicate neither where Jacob was nor what he was up to that moment. "Nothing!" she proclaimed frustratingly, "Nothing."

Nearing a feeling of frantic, anxiety setting in fiercely, Naomi began opening drawers of his custom rainbow walnut wood desk; it was a gift from Naomi on their tenth year anniversary. Having found a custom wood shop near Seattle, she had designed the diameters of the desk for the space it could fit, and drew the detailed edging the wood maker would later engrave onto the piece. It was marvelous, cut to a perfect masculine curve, the deep browns and greens swimming in unison above the almond-coffee and pumpkin colors that lined flawlessly below. The legs were designed with a swaying curve, as though a glass pillar had melted here and there, representing their imperfectly-perfect marriage, Naomi thought. It was coated with a wood polish, no artificial staining, and sealed with a clear coat to highlight all those natural colors of the once was tree that she visualized standing tall at the ocean's cliff and strong against all winds. Loose items rolled front to back as she pulled open the drawers, pawing at papers.

She found a business card from Tommy Krindle; "strange," she thought, "only a name," though a hand written phone number was scribbled beneath. There was also a folder hidden in the back of the drawer containing some medical bills Jacob had obviously been hiding from her . . . figuring Naomi had enough on her plate with all the stacking bills they still hadn't had enough money to pay off, Jacob had started hiding them, to ease her stress. Of course, finding them now only added to her stress, and she wondered even more what else Jacob could be hiding from her.

Exhausted, Naomi collapsed her tall, thin body onto his thick brown leather chair, letting the bills fall from her hands to the floor. She closed her eyes, and massaged her hands on the roughed leather material, hoping for any hint of calm to take over her. Lifting open her eyelids, Naomi's glance came across their phone bill; another item he had kept from her, for the house line. Now, standing in a lean, balancing her quick awkward stance with one hand still on the warmth of the arm of Jacob's leather chair; she loved the way it smelled—she swooped up the phone bill, stood up straight, and ran out of the den, grabbing the cordless phone on her way to the kitchen.

Sitting at the kitchen's island counter, laptop open, Naomi signed into their online account for their home phone service; she paid almost all of their bills online now days and her mind drifted momentarily to the stack of check books in her study that she ever so seldom used—and then read over the phone log. First: Jacob's mobile number, the next reflected the number that called before he left the house yesterday. Naomi dialed the number.

A man's voice answered. He had a thick accent and Naomi thought to herself, "Alabama?"

"Dispatcher, how can I assist you today, Mr. Willem?"

Disappointment taking hold, feeling as though her voice had fallen shaky, she slowly and awkwardly responded, "Uh, ooh-hello . . . this is Naomi Willem. I'm a little concerned . . . you see . . . well, my husband hasn't come home yet. I know this probably seems silly, but . . . well, he left in a hurry last night, and I haven't heard from him since. I just want to know if he's okay. Do you happen to know where I can find him?"

There was a long pause before Alabama on the other end of the line responded; Naomi knowing in her gut that he was the key to all the answers she needed, she heard a deep raspy intake of air, a breathing only a chain smoking man seems to have the ability to accomplish an expression of annoyance and impatience without a word, and then he explained in his thick, cocky, Alabama-accent, "Umm . . . Well, I am sorry, Ma'am, but this is a private line, and all information given to me is held in strict confidentiality. I'm sorry, I just can't help you. Good-bye, Mrs. Willem."

Before the man could hang up, Naomi retorted with a sense of urgency, "Wait, no, please, wait! Just tell me, is he there? Is Jacob at his office?"

"Ma'am, I am sorry, but I really do not know. It's not my job to keep tabs on anyone's whereabouts." Catching his own sense of sarcasm, he paused before adding, "What I can do is offer you Mr. Willem's superior's name and transfer you there."

"Oh, yes, please do. Is that Mr. Borgam?"

"Yes, Ma'am, it is. Please hold on the line." The man transferred Naomi to Clint Borgam's phone.

"Borgam."

The noise in the background was loud, and it was difficult for Naomi to hear him answer.

"Hello, Borgam here!" Clint answered again impatiently.

"Yes, Clint, hello! I can barely hear you . . . I'm sorry to be calling, but do you know where I can find Jacob?"

Borgam replied sharply, "Who is this?"

"Ooh, I'm so sorry, it's late, and I'm worried I've lost my head a little. Clint, this is Naomi, Jacob's wife. Do you . . . do you know where he is?"

"No, I'm sorry, Naomi, I don't. I've been wondering the same thing, you know. Is something wrong?"

"Well, you see these explosions happened, and Jacob got a late call last night. He left for the office, but he's still not home, and, well . . . I'm really worried."

"Explosions? How did you know?"

"Know what?" Naomi asked.

There was a silence that sent cold chills up Naomi's spine, until Clint Borgam finally responded, "Nothing, I must have misunderstood you, Mrs. Willem. You just calm down now. I assure you, Jacob is fine. We will find him."

CHAPTER 15

INN AT THE E.R.

"Rose, I need you. Can you come to the house?" Naomi, nearing tears and then realizing it was not her own tears she was sensing, listened for a response on the other end of the phone.

"I can't, Naomi . . . I'm at the hospital."

"The hospital? Why? Are you alright?'

"Naomi, it's my son. He is very ill."

"Your son?"

"Yes . . . Will. He had a horrible night. He woke with a high fever and shakes that were uncontrollable. We've been here for hours already. We're just waiting for the doctor to come back with the news. Nurses are trying to make him as comfortable as he can possibly be, but he's not alert, Naomi. He's . . ." breaking down, Rose began to sob, "He's covered in tubes, and unconscious. I've . . . He's . . . It's never been this bad, Naomi. I don't know what I'll do if . . ." Crying uncontrollably, Rose's words were hard to understand, and Naomi interjected: "Honey, I am so sorry. I didn't know . . . I'm leaving right now! What hospital?"

"St. Jude's, downtown," Rose answered exhaustively; in between sobs, with mascara burning into her tear filled eyes, she had not realized she had just welcomed her dear friend, Naomi, there beside her, beside him. "What have I done, no," she cried out, but it was too late, Naomi had already disconnected. "No . . ." Rose whispered desperately.

When Naomi pulled into the hospital emergency parking garage, the lot was full. She finally found the last available spot on the fifth floor, and had to wedge her Nissan 350Z between a nearly diagonally parked old Cadillac on the left, and a small Honda on the right. Pressing the brake, she quickly set the gear to Park, holding her keys in one hand, and grabbed her pocket book with the other. As she shut the car door she remembered the paper bag of goodies she bought on the way at the gas station, for Rose; comfort junk-foods and crossword puzzles while waiting at the hospital was a necessity she knew all too well from all the long nights at the emergency room with Jacob. She paused a moment at the car and wrote Rose a note and placed it in the bag.

Running towards the elevator, she set the alarm of her Z, and waited impatiently for the elevator to reach her. After what seemed an eternity, she gave up, and descended the staircase next to the elevator instead.

Inside, she asked at the reception desk what room to find—she couldn't remember the boy's name. She explained her friend, Rose Carson, was the mother, and she knew the boy was almost coma-like, but she wasn't sure where to go. The heavy set woman behind the tall desk took her dear'ol'time looking up the information in the computer that Naomi had provided to the best of her memory, and without a glance at Naomi nor a response, she offered a final word, "E.R."

"Oh-well, I thank you," Naomi responded snottily, slightly shaking her head, she proceeded down the long hallway to the emergency room, where she had to wait for visitors to be called. It seemed these places relished on making people wait, and that always irked Naomi so. She followed the rules though, put up no fuss, as she knew from past experience all that would do is cause the waiting time to be even longer.

An hour and fifteen minutes passed in a way that felt like someone hit the slow motion key on the DVD player, and Naomi's time amongst the sickly, drunken, and injured waiting to hear their name called, was the movie. Finally a staunch-built short woman opened the E.R. doors, wearing flowered scrubs and the ever so official name tag attached to bright red yarn around her pudgy neck; she yelled out, "VISITORS!" A group of people quickly squirmed to form a line in front of this woman as though she was someone famous ready to sign autographs. Naomi followed, and as each person passed through the heavy double doors, they announced their intended visitation, and so Naomi did the same.

She looked at the nurse and said, "Little boy, Carson." The nurse gave Naomi a soft smile, and said, "Follow me," to the group. Leading them through the patient waiting room; more like an overcrowded hall filled with obvious fist-fought and bloodied drunks in slumber hunched over chairs and appearing ready to fall to the white and gray speckled linoleum floor, and then through the next set of heavy double doors that opened automatically with a quick swipe of the nurse's highly technical name badge hanging from that bright red yarn.

The nurse escorted the group of people to their designated friends and family for visiting. Naomi was last. The nurse turned to her and said, "Carson, right?"

"That's right," replied Naomi.

"He was just moved upstairs about thirty minutes ago. Fourth floor, room . . ." the nurse flipped through the papers attached to a clipboard she held in her arms, ". . . 421. You can actually access that area without coming through E.R. though, did you know that?"

"The reception desk told me to come here, but the wait was so long, I . . ."

"That's okay, I'll show you. I need a break anyway."

The nurse escorted Naomi, walking a few feet in front of her the entire way, through empty halls, and elevators occupied only with doctors and other staff. Naomi realized she had never been in this part of this hospital. It seemed baron, empty, so lifeless.

The nurse turned her head back slightly and must have noticed Naomi's curious expression. "This part of the hospital is off limits until the construction for the addition is completed, so you won't be able to come back this way, okay?"

"Alright," Naomi answered.

Finally, they reached the fourth floor, and the nurse pointed which way for Naomi to continue on her own.

Down another long hallway, passing what seemed like far too many staff people that seemed not to know where they were headed; exhausted expressions amongst their faces, taking their time to get to where ever they were headed as they knew this was probably the last moment to have to themselves that they would have for the rest of their shift. Every other few feet were more staff persons, rolling carts loaded of cleaning supplies. Then she walked around a long counter occupied with more staff, nurses, and doctors standing, reading clipboards, until Naomi came to room 421. "Finally," she announced, and poked her head through the doorway, knocking softly on the open wooden door that had so many signs attached to it; one wouldn't know what to read first.

"Naomi!" Rose stood and embraced her friend she had not seen in nearly two decades. She did not want to let go. Tears streamed down both of their cheeks, and Naomi let out a soft giggle, smiling at her friend, kissing her cold cheek, thinking how great, though tired, she looked after all this time. Smiling, a warm expression upon her poised-statuette face, Naomi handed out the paper bag, "Here's some soul-food and games to keep you occupied."

Taking the bag, and turning towards her son's bedside, Rose set the goodies on the rolling table next to him, and placed her hand in Naomi's, "Thank you for coming."

They sat in silence for several minutes, holding hands; Naomi softly caressed Rose's back in a soothing gesture.

"Rose . . . how old is—I am so sorry, I can't remember his name."

Terrified of what was to come, Rose's eyes filled with guilt, and she began to cry. Long, silent, sobs of despair. She could hardly breathe. Her heart was racing, and her chest shuddered with each breath. She appeared faint as her face had flushed colorless.

"Naomi . . . this—" she took in a deep breath through her nose, "This is Will, Willem O'Brien Carson. He's almost fifteen. The doctors knew he'd be ill born even while I was pregnant. He's been sick since he was a baby, and I—"

Naomi felt a crisp shock take over composure, as though she was kicked in the gut. She held up her hand, palm facing Rose, as to say, Stop. "Say no more," she managed as she felt her chest collapse inwardly.

Naomi walked to Will's bedside, her eyes looking at him from tiptoe to head's top. She thought to herself, "Willem? Jacob's son . . . Jacob and Rose, but, how . . . When? Cambridge," she remembered. She placed her hand on Will's forehead, and leaned close to kiss his temple. "He's burning up. What's wrong with him, Rose?"

"Cancer . . . he had a bad reaction to the chemo treatment last night. Naomi, I . . ." Rose still sobbing, head twitching side to side with nerves as though shivering after swimming in a frigid lake; could say no more.

Naomi ran her fingers through Will's thinning hair, taking in the sight of this thin, handsome, flush-faced boy covered in tubes, hooked to oxygen, and attached to a heart monitor. Inhaling a slight breath, sniffling softly, she swallowed her saliva; hard it went down passed her throat, as though poisoned and her lungs feared it so.

Not knowing what else to say, she gathered her pocket book and keys in one hand, and stood facing Rose who stood up slowly in front of her. With all her might and anger inside her, the hurt that Naomi felt now slapped across Rose's face, and Naomi's palm stung with pain. She turned to leave the room. Rose followed, holding her cheek still, calling out, "Wait, Naomi . . . Please! Wait! Let me explain!"

Naomi picked up pace, never looking behind as she felt her tears taking over her composure even more. She reached her arm back behind her while running, raised up the palm of her hand, and replied, "There's nothing more to explain, Rose . . ."

Around the corner Naomi disappeared through a doorway and hurried down the stairway adjacent the elevators she had ridden up on to reunite with her friend, to comfort her while her son so ill . . . "Her son, Jacob's son . . . Oh-god," she cried out, "My son . . . He should've been my son!" Tears of pain stopped her in her footsteps. She collapsed on the stairway in disbelief from a pain she had never known before. "Why?" she called out, and the echo of her voice returned to her, "Why?" her own voice whispering back in her ear.

She held tight the white-painted iron-hand-railing, so cold, and pulled herself upward. She didn't see Rose above her a flight, watching her, waiting for the right moment, waiting for the right words to come to her to go and comfort her friend, waiting, as she had been doing for the last fifteen years since Jacob had met her at that pub there in Ballard.

As Naomi neared the exit of the hospital on the main floor, she realized she was completely turned around. Gaining her composure, she shook her head quickly side to side, wiped away the tears against her cheeks with her hands, and looked for the directory signs to the E.R. parking garage.

Rose followed from a distance behind as not to be seen. She shadowed Naomi down the long halls, and corridors, until reaching back to the chaos of the emergency waiting room. It was there that Naomi heard a voice of a man moaning loudly; so familiar. She turned her head to see this moaning man being rushed through those same double doors that the nice staunch-nurse had led her and other visitors through.

"Jacob?" Naomi called out. Could she be sure? With so many people surrounding him, and Naomi so very tired, could she be sure that was her husband lying there? She quickly walked towards the moaning man and before she could get close enough, the huge swinging automatic double doors closed in front of her.

Knock-knock-knock; she pounded with her palm on the receptionist's glass surrounded desk, "I'm with them, open the door!" Surprisingly, the receptionist did just that, and the automatic doors swung wide open once again.

Darting through the mess of people, and trying to stay close enough to the moaning man on the stretcher surrounded by paramedics from an ambulance team, Naomi finally had a chance for a good look. She saw him, Jacob, her husband, bloodied, pale, and unconscious. The team of people quickly out of reach behind closed glass doors, a nurse swung the cotton curtain attached to rollers along the ceiling, shut, and Naomi could no longer see. Standing there in the walkway, hand clinched onto her pocket book held to her stomach, the other hand firmly across her mouth holding in her gasps of disbelief, her eyes squinted with fear, until a nurse touched her shoulder, "Are you alright, Ma'am? Can I help you with something?"

Naomi stood frozen in silence until finally she felt the touch of the nurse's hand, "Ma'am! Ma'am, hello, are you alright?"

Pointing straight ahead, "That's . . . that's my husband. Do you know what happened?"

"I'm not sure. Why don't you have a seat in the waiting room and I'll find out for you." The nurse escorted Naomi to a small lobby by the overcrowded patient waiting room filled with sleeping drunks.

Rose had seen Naomi follow, and waited in the front lobby. She told the receptionist she was a friend of the man they just brought in and asked what was wrong. The receptionist told her she would have to wait in the waiting room and that visitors would be called upon soon.

"My son is admitted here on the fourth floor, in room 421. Is there any way you can call me there?"

"Are you related?"

"No, I just told you I am a friend of the family."

"Then you can come back and wait for visitors to be called when you feel like it, Ma'am."

Frustrated, Rose thought about returning to Will's bedside. She would check on Jacob later, she told herself, besides she didn't want to upset Naomi any more than she already had.

Though it seemed like a decade later, a nurse eventually appeared in the lobby. "Mrs. Willem?" Naomi stood and followed her to Jacob's room. He was bandaged nearly head to toe, hooked to oxygen, some machine that appeared to be working his lungs for him, and IV drips. Naomi felt her knees go weak, so she sat in a distant chair in his room, and watched him bewilderedly while he struggled to breathe.

"How could you?" she said aloud knowing Jacob would not be able to answer.

Naomi stood, heartbroken, staring down at him on that hospital bed, covered in blood and scrapes all over the exposed skin on his legs, chest, arms, and face. She realized in that moment that she did not know this near-dead-man lying in front of her that she called her husband, and she felt alone, so very alone.

Awhile later, Rose came to visit Jacob. When she arrived, she realized Naomi was still there. "Why wouldn't she be?" she thought to herself. Not wanting to be seen, she stood with her back against the wall beside the room, pulled her cell phone out in hand, acting like she was texting or playing a game as to not appear suspicious just standing there. She was out of sight but in hearing distance.

A nurse rushed by and entered the room wearing protective gear. She told Naomi that she would be required to do so as well. "Here," handing Naomi a plastic bag stuffed full of blue cloth, "put these on in there," the nurse pointed towards a bathroom in the hall.

Ignoring the nurse's instruction to leave the room, Naomi stood next to Jacob, and asked her, "What happened?" all while slipping the blue cotton paper-like coverall over her head, and straightened it along her waist. Next, the pants, gloves, hair net, and face cover.

"Car accident off of 9th Street, downtown, I guess. The EMT said he rolled his truck. It's totaled, Mrs. Willem. He has a fractured collar bone, and broke several bones in his legs. His left arm was completely crushed, and his right lung's collapsed. Your husband is lucky to be alive. Other than his injuries, though, he seems to be very ill. Mrs. Willem, does your husband have any medical conditions, or illnesses we need to know about?"

"Well, yes, actually, he's been getting worse over the last few months. His doctor can't seem to figure it out. Body shakes, sweats at night, strange twinges, and severe pain throughout his body. He gets horrible migraines, has a hard time sleeping, and sometimes his veins appear to turn black. When that happens, he usually faints from the pain, and we end up at the E.R. in Darrington." Naomi paused, "but why the protective wear?"

"Blood tests came back. Doctor's orders! Just waiting for remaining results, I'm guessing. We'll have to do more blood tests, too, so you just sit tight. We'll keep you posted as we find out more, okay? Do you need anything, how about some coffee or juice?" The nurse replied optimistically.

"No, I'm fine, but thank you."

As the nurse turned to leave the room, she looked back as though she had forgotten something. "Mrs. Willem? Where does your husband work?"

"He's an engineer. He works for Crione Agency in Darrington."

A concerned look came over the nurse's face as she disappeared through the doors, and over to the nursing station. Naomi leaned slightly forward so she could see out and stretched to hear, but the nurse was too far away now to make anything out of it. Shortly after, a young man wearing a white jacket and name badge attached to his breast pocket entered the room. "Mrs. Willem? My name is Doctor Herrera. Other than what Nurse Peggy has already explained, there's really not much more I can tell you now, except that we need to do more tests and run your husband's blood again. I'm afraid I just don't have any answers for you yet."

"What are you talking about? What answers do you think I need? What's going on? The nurse already told me about Jacob's accident, and his injuries. I know they're severe, but he will heal, right?"

"Mrs. Willem . . . I don't know how to tell you this. I just don't have all the answers yet, but it seems apparent that your husband has been exposed to a form of radiation. We'll have to quarantine him until we know more. You are welcome to wait in the lobby in the meantime."

Rose was still listening outside the door; she heard Naomi being told to leave and that there was something about radiation being involved with Jacob's condition. Rose thought of Will, and knew she could not risk any more exposures to him. Worriedly she returns to her son's bedside four floors up.

Naomi, sitting in the lobby again, thought of Will and Rose, and then everything nurse Peggy had said to her; "9th Street, Downtown."

"He was headed to Rose," breathless, feeling despair set its foot firmly inside of her heart once more, she stood, and left to go home.

Late that night, Naomi poured herself a hot bath; running her head under the facet to wet her long hair. She needed to feel the water on her face, caressing its silky touch upon her skin. She welcomed the warmth of the water to engulf her, to embrace her weary energies, and massage her heavy eyelids. Waiting for the tub to fill, not bothering to towel her soaked hair, she walked to the kitchen, pulled a deep crystal wine glass from the cupboard, filled it to the rim with Merlot, and proceeded to take from her cupboard, also, her sleeping pills. Crushing all of the little yellow color-coated pills with a butter knife over a piece of mail, she slowly dropped the grainy particles into her wine glass, watching the white formula coagulate together until dropping heavily to the bottom of her glass. She held it high towards the light fixture above, looking through this white form resting peacefully at its bottom and encompassed with the rich colors of Merlot spilling over onto her hand and down her wrist, she drank it in one long gulp.

Naomi walked to her study, ignoring her bath, and the water she could hear pouring over the sides of the tub onto their custom tiled floor, and slowly stripped her body naked from the trappings of her clothes, filthy, she felt so filthy.

She began to paint. Her hair was still wet, and now dripping down her back onto her dry skin. The drops were soaking in . . . soaking into her pores, and she could feel its motion, the sensation transcending her into a stupor. She paints . . . her thoughts were unattached, looming above her, outside of her, everywhere but within her. On the canvass, she painted a deep red background blanketing the form of a baby hovering freely in a fetus position, painted white, and holding in his hand, his mother's lock of red hair.

She laid on her chaise, observing her painting, feeling at last, a peace that had filled the room and comforted her naked skin. Whispering aloud, "Beautiful is love . . . even if it is questionable." She closed her eyes, letting loose the paintbrush still in hand; it fell to the floor, kissing its paint covered bristles on the dark-wood-stained floor. Silence filled the room. She felt herself give into the pull of slumber, as she half laid; half slumped there on her chaise. She allowed her arms to drop free beside her and fell asleep, feeling the peace and relief take over her mind as she intended never to wake.

CHAPTER 16

SEVER TIES

The following morning, Clint Borgam sat at his desk at Crione Agency. He made all the necessary phone calls; status update to Frank Calister, check in call to Naomi Willem who did not answer, and a phone call to Tommy Krindle's wife, Tami. Thinking he needed to cover his tracks, he asked Tami if she had heard from Tommy and to have him call when he came home. Clueless as to the fact that Borgam had stabbed and burned her husband's body on the mountain the day before in the containment room, Tami told him about her conversation with Naomi Willem. She told Clint Borgam that he should try talking with the Willems. "They know too much," she told him.

Following orders from Frank Calister, Clint Borgam proceeded to make calls to search down and find the whereabouts of Jacob Willem. He had not been heard from since he was at the project site the evening of the last explosions. After numerous calls to local police departments, and hospitals, Borgam found Jacob at St. Jude's Hospital downtown near Ballard, WA.

The nurse he spoke with indicated the severity of Jacob's pending condition, fractured bones, and collapsed lung after explaining Jacob had been in a car accident the night before. She told Borgam these things given that he had lied to her and stated he was Jacob's father, Richard Willem, visiting from Nebraska and not able to locate his son or his wife, so he, of course, had grown worried. Feeling sympathetic to Clint's, aka: Richard's, story, the nurse was much more informative than protocol would normally allow.

Clint headed downtown to Ballard to have a visit with Jacob. He needed to know firsthand just how severe his condition was, and to figure out a way to resolve his tie to the project site.

In the meantime, Frank Calister called Clint Borgam on his mobile phone. He told him that detectives were asking too many questions, and that they would be headed to Clint's place later the same day to question him regarding the project site rumors. "This situation is getting out of control, Borgam. Sever all ties. I should not have to repeat myself again," Calister ordered.

Along the way to the hospital, Clint stopped at his house and disguised himself as Jacob's father, Richard Willem. When Clint arrived at St. Jude's, nurses told him that Jacob was not allowed visitors due to his condition and that he had been quarantined. Clint, insisting to see his "son," told the nurse he didn't care what his condition was, "I will see my son one way or another!"

After minutes of debating, Clint having perfected the art of persuasion learned from Frank Calister, he eventually was allowed a few minutes of visiting as long as he agreed to dress in the protective wear.

When Clint entered Jacob's room, he saw very quickly that Jacob was not alert, and that he was hooked up to a machine working his lungs for him. "This will be easier than expected," Clint thought to himself. He approached Jacob's bedside, and stood before him a man now detached from human decency. That moment, a slight glimpse of the fifteen plus years they had worked together, flooded Clint's memory like a flash flood he could not control. Several minutes had passed when Jacob suddenly began to show signs of consciousness. Clint snapped back into the moment, remembering his orders, and his purpose for being there. It was a part of the job, and he wasn't about to risk his career on the possibility of being held responsible for the accident at the Glacier Point Peak Pass project site.

Pulling from his coat pocket an anesthetic-soaked cloth, a chemical he had created at home made from a narcotic, bleach, and the opium poppy, he held the cloth firmly across Jacob's face. The fumes quickly caused him to pass out. Clint pinched Jacob's oxygen tube tight, and leaned down close to his ear, whispering, "Go ahead, Boy, sleep now. Willem, I am going to pin this whole mess on a dead guy." Jacob's heart monitors began beeping slowly; to a pace that alarms nursing staff of a slowed heart rate and lack of oxygen.

In the interim, Rose Carson was still at the hospital with her son, Will.

She had headed down to the first floor to the cafeteria for a bite to eat, and on the way she thought of Jacob lying in the emergency room. So, instead she headed down the long corridor and hallways to E.R. to see if she could visit with him now, hoping Naomi was not there still, and was already awaiting visitors to be called before Borgam had barged through the doors. Rose had noticed the chaos and yelling when a man had rushed into the emergency room, but really paid no attention to it, other than being annoyed at how rude some people were. She thought he should have to wait just like the rest of them.

When the large automatic doors opened after a nurse escorted a group of visitors in, Rose was led to that long counter of nurse staff and doctors near Jacob's room. She was told the same thing that Clint Borgam had been told just moments ago, so she complied but asked if she could just peak her head in and see him. The nurse agreed and whispered secretively that Rose was not to disturb them though, as Jacob's father was in there now visiting with him. "I can get in a lot of trouble for letting him have visitors, so just please don't be long, okay?" The nurse confided.

"His father? Richard is here?" Rose inquired.

She walked to Jacob's room, having already placed her face mask on that the nurse had provided, and saw a man standing over Jacob. It appeared he was whispering something in his ear.

"Richard?" Rose called out, opening the door firmly against the wall behind it.

Clint Borgam startled to hear Richard's name, stood up quickly and scurried out of the room; his shoulder knocking hard against Rose's, which nearly knocked her to the floor. She caught herself, and immediately yelled out towards to the nurse station, "That's not Richard Willem!"

The nurse rushed into Jacob's room while another called for Security. Clint managed to slip out a back door through the closed off section of the hospital that was under construction. Security eventually lost him, unable to keep up.

Running to the parking garage as quickly as he could, Clint's mind was racing, feeling satisfied that the woman, whoever she may have been, he thought, had not seen his face with all the required protective clothes and face mask he had on. "Ah, shit, what about the nurse? Calister's going to have my head for this one," he said to himself.

Stripping off the cotton blue clothes as he approached his truck, and having slowed down after sprinting out of sight from the security guards,

Clint thought about how he was going to have to figure out how to clean his hands of this sudden new mess he had just created. "How can I blame Willem for all this now?" he worried aloud to himself.

Reaching his truck, he sped out of the parking garage, and dreaded the next call he would have to make.

"Calister, Borgam here. Mission was interrupted. May be witnesses. After target stabilized and in new location, mission will be completed." Speaking like a robot writing a book report; Clint tried to assure Calister he had everything under control.

Frank Calister was furious, and replied simply, "I'll do it myself." He hung up without another word spoken.

Panicked, and angry at himself, Clint retreated to the nearest local bar he came across; fearing if he went home, the detectives would be there to question him.

"Scotch on the rocks, double," he murmured to the bartender as he sat alone on a stool at the bartender's counter, alone in a dark, muggy, half lit pub, and having no clue as to what was in store for him next.

Chapter 17

Omaha

Frank Calister knew Clint Borgam enjoyed his scotch, as they had shared a many over the years they had worked together. Calister drove to St. Jude's hospital, slowing down outside the emergency room entrance, his silver Mercedes-Benz SLR-722 idled momentarily, and then with precise decisiveness, he quickly accelerated. Exiting off the hospital property, he headed in the direction of Clint Borgam's house. Knowing Borgam would have stopped for a drink just after they spoke, he intended on tracking his last move.

Calister did just that and spotted Borgam's old orange Chevy pickup truck in the parking lot of a pub. Calister parked outside the front door, and entered the bar. He approached a very inebriated Borgam and told him quietly in his ear, "Let's go, Borgam. I have something to show you."

Staggering from his bar-stool, Borgam replied in a drunken slur, "Frankie, my man . . . sit down, cool off, have a scotch with me. Bartender! Give us a round."

They sat and drank their scotch. Calister paid the bill, and gathered up Borgam under an arm, and assisted him out the bar to his Mercedes.

They drove an hour and a half, which Borgam slept mostly through, until Calister came to a brisk stop at the once was tunnel entrance of the mountain. Blinking several times, eyebrows raised, Borgam tried to focus out the window to see where they were. Calister was already out of the car, and opening Borgam's car door. He helped Borgam out of the passenger seat and they walked slowly to the boulders now covering the tunnel. Calister told him he wanted to see the damage to the tunnel entrance.

Stuttering, Borgam drunkenly tried to explain that he had already handled the mess at the site, "See, I took care of it," he slurred, spit splashing against Calister's chest and chin.

"There's one thing you forgot, Borgam," Calister replied in a sinisterly low toned voice, turning his back to Borgam.

Finding it difficult to stand up straight, Borgam's body wavered back and forth, until he caught himself with one hand against Calister's shoulder. Calister turned slowly toward him again, appearing motionless.

Two shots were fired at Borgam's stomach in close range. Frank Calister rolled Borgam's dead body off the side of the mountain. Clint Borgam, his body lifeless and tumbling down the mountainside, broke branches, and left splats of blood here and there. Calister stood above, a hunter watching his kill fade away, laughed out loud when he realized that wasn't the cleanest kill he had ever made. "Getting rusty," he told himself, amused by the apparent amateur move he had just made, shook his head in a matter to shrug off the obvious, and returned to his car.

He sped to his office, made some calls, and booked his private jet. First stop, Omaha, Nebraska. Second stop, Paris, France. He'd have to brief his client on the whereabouts of the warheads, assure them the site had been secured, even though he had no idea the extensive damage Borgam probably caused when he sealed off the tunnel. Nonetheless, he would brief Richard Willem on the situation, and they would fly to Paris together to secure their account, a group of modern day guerrillas with the FCRN; French Club for the Right to produce Nuclear warheads. He packed a small carry on, grabbed his cash and some documents from the safe, and left the office.

Next stop, the Willems' house. He reloaded his gun still sitting in the passenger seat.

When he reached Jacob and Naomi Willem's house, Frank Calister parked along the road at the edge of the property, aside their driveway. He noticed Jacob's Dodge truck was not there, and remembered Borgam had told him Jacob's truck had been in an accident. He wondered who the other car was for, as there were two cars parked side by side in their driveway.

Calister stepped out of his car, walked slowly past the two cars, and then quickly to the front door of the house. The door was open, and as he stepped in, he slipped his black leather gloves over his hands, and screwed the SOCOM kjm9 Silencer onto the barrel of his silver Beretta handgun.

"Anyone home?" he called out calmly, gun in hand, as he walked through the hall passed the den, and into the kitchen. Stepping softly, in long strides, Calister continued towards the back of the house, glanced through the window onto the porch, and saw a woman knelt down on the deck floor next to Naomi Willem who was lying in her lawn lounger. The woman appeared to be holding something to Naomi's forehead, and they were holding hands.

After leaving Jacob and Naomi's house, Frank Calister; tall, cool, calm, powerful, and confident—headed towards the airstrip to board his first flight. He knew he needed to ease the recipient's mind of the now buried warheads, but needed to make his appearance in Omaha first. He proceeded to the plane and took a seat in his private jet.

As the loud roaring engines warmed themselves, the slight vibration in Calister's seat massaged his overworked bones. He glared his eyes narrow, focused, preparing himself for the conversation to be had with Richard Willem.

Chapter 18

Take Care of Her

After landing in Omaha, Richard Willem escorted Frank Calister to his house, where his wife, Florence, had prepared them a delicious supper. After eating and visiting for a while, Richard and Frank descended to the basement where Richards's home office was. He had his private experiment room there that he was anxious to show off to Calister. There, they discussed the status of the project site at Glacier Point Peak, and the separate flights Calister had booked for them to Paris the following week. Richard Willem showed Calister the blueprints for the new holding tanks so they could have the bio terrorist nuclear warheads delivered undetectable across seas to the new project site in France. Frank Calister explained that Clint Borgam, "The dumb ass," he told Richard, "He blew up the entire tunnel's entrance. I'm sure police will be there soon, too. We'll let them do the heavy work digging it all out, and when timing is opportune, we'll send our men back in to retrieve remaining weapons. Borgam was supposed to relocate the tanks into the containment room, so hopefully that is exactly what he did before blowing up the place. We should have a few salvaged shells, several warheads, and two tanks with the completed nuclear bombs in their casings still secured."

"Did you take care of Naomi as I instructed?" Richard Willem interrupted.

Calister responded with a nod.

"What about Borgam?"

Again, Calister nodded, "It's all handled, Richard. All ties are severed. Jacob's crew was trapped inside the tunnel during one of the explosions, and I sent my best men in to clean up the mess after all that happened. Looks like all links are unidentifiable. Media's all over this one, though.

Police have already been calling, trying to track down everyone to take into questioning. So far, I've been able to avoid them for the most part."

"Calister, I know you hired Jacob because we're friends, you followed my orders, and I trust you've had him in your best interest through this project, but I have to say, I am discouraged and incredibly disappointed with these outcomes. I don't understand how the structures could have been faulty, only the hands that built them can make mistakes. The blueprints were sound. Jacob did everything right. He can't be blamed for this. I can't lose another child, Frank." Richard spoke candidly to his longtime friend.

Jacob Willem's youngest sister, Jennifer, was 15 years old when he was a junior at MIT in Cambridge, MA. His father, Richard, had called Jacob one night to inform him of his sister's passing after a fatal car accident she had been in. "Jennifer had an argument with your mom," Richard told Jacob. "She sneaked out of the house last night afterward, and took your mom's mini-van. She left a note that she was going to Cambridge to be with you. She said you told her that Naomi left you, and that you'd need the company. Why didn't you tell us, Son?" Richard had asked of him.

Jacob didn't know what to respond to first. He explained what had happened between him and Rose Carson, and Naomi finding out, then broke down crying because of the news of his sister. "I never thought Jennifer would actually come, Dad. I swear. Is that what the argument was about with Mom, coming to see me? Oh-Dad . . . I'm so . . . I'm so ashamed."

"That doesn't matter, Son. She drove off the side of the road . . . she hit a tree . . . wrapped the van completely around it like a . . . like a taco. She was . . . dead on impact . . ." Richard Willem broke down that very moment, sobbing like only a childless parent knows. Talking with Jacob always allowed himself to let go. He was reminded of his faults, his imperfections, and the reality of now having survived a life longer than his own daughter. "This isn't the order of things, Son . . . Ooh, dear-God . . . why did He let this happen?"

Jacob and his father, Richard, cried together for the first time in their lives. Even when Naomi lost the baby, and Jacob was so distraught, Richard remained the strong one; always the oak of the family. This, however, this he could not handle. Richard grew angry with God, and his wife, all while Florence grew withdrawn to her own solitude and self-blame.

They had nothing to hold each other up anymore, and Richard took to drinking instead of praying. It was years later before he and Florence really spoke . . . spoke of anything sound, anything of importance, and especially of their precious Jennifer, lost too soon in this life. All the years in between were a charade with raising their remaining children, and grandchildren. Richard's work took up even more of his time and dedication than it had ever consumed before. Anything to hide the pain they felt, anything to forget the loss of a child.

Frank Calister again nodded. "It'll work itself out, Richard. Don't you worry about it. I have everything under control."

". . . and Krindle? What has Tommy Krindle to say of all of this?" Richard asked.

"Can you believe I haven't heard from Tommy through this entire episode? I have no idea where that man has sneaked off to, to tell you the truth. I don't think he's a concern though. He'd just tell me to get the situation under control, and I have. We have," he responded. "I'm sure he's off on his boat somewhere drunk and passed out with some whore."

Calister hesitated before continuing, taking in a deep breath, he cleared his throat, and flexed his shoulders up and down quickly to release the tension, "Richard, I have something else I need to tell you."

"Well, what is it, Frank?"

"It's your son, Jacob. He was in a horrible accident and flipped his truck downtown near Ballard, outside of Seattle. He's also been exposed to nuclear leaks, the spills from the punctured tanks—they've caused him to be quite ill these past months. For years, he's been inhaling and working in those poisons . . . without even knowing it. Apparently, he's not doing too well, Buddy, I'm sorry. He's been hospitalized, and is under quarantine. He'll pull through, I'm sure, but I don't know if he'll ever work again." Calister did not dare tell Richard of his plans to eliminate Jacob from the picture. That time would come, he thought, that time will come.

Tears swelling up in Richard Willem's eyes, the guilt he now felt in his stomach for the mark he'd placed on Naomi's head, he felt as though he could hurl this moment, and dropped to a chair as though he'd suddenly been kicked by a horse's hove to the groin. He whispered, "We've got to get me to him, Frank. Now."

CHAPTER 19

LET ME EXPLAIN

Rose's son had stabilized, and she was given the orders from the doctor that it would be okay to take Willem back home to continue his treatments.

As she gathered their things, she noticed that Willem's color in his face had returned and how almost normal, kid-like, he looked . . . healthy. "We're going to get through this, Son . . . Gosh, Will, you look so much like your dad," Rose told Willem.

On their way home from the hospital, after a long silence had passed, Willem asked his mom if she was alright, and who his dad was, and who the lady in his hospital room was the other day.

"You saw her?" Rose asked surprisingly.

Willem nodded, "Mom, why have you never told me anything about my dad? Who am I? Why don't you ever treat me like a person? I'm more than a boy with cancer, you know? I'm your son, and if I have a dad out there, I want to know about him, alright?" he continued in frustration.

Rose began to cry. Something she had become quite accustomed to these days, and told Willem, "Son, please don't get yourself worked up. Let me explain, okay? I'll tell you everything you want to know! But, right now, we need to go visit someone."

"Who?" Willem asked in a monotone voice, trying to appear tougher than his emotions really felt inside of him.

"Your Dad's wife. Naomi, she was my best friend since we were younger than you are now. She is the one that came to see you, too. You see, Will, Naomi and I . . ." and Rose continued in length about the details of how she and Naomi met in elementary school, how Rose would visit her own dad in Seattle each summer, and return to tell Naomi all of her exciting adventures.

She told Willem how Naomi and his father, Jacob Willem, met and that they moved to Cambridge where his dad had gone to MIT. Rose explained that while they lived there, Naomi had become pregnant with their first baby, but had problems and they lost the baby, telling Willem that Naomi could never have children of her own after that. She confessed to her son that she offered to be a surrogate carrier for her friends, and explained to Willem what that meant. She then confessed that that didn't happen, and that she and his father, Jacob Willem, had had sex one night so she could carry his child for them. She explained she was supposed to give Willem to Jacob and Naomi after he was born, but instead she kept him to herself. She explained everything, and the current situation meaning that Naomi had never known until now, and that Jacob, also, was sick in the hospital.

The drive to Naomi and Jacob's house seemed to go by too quickly for Willem, while Rose rambled out a lifetime of history in an hour's drive, and she told him she still had so much to explain, but right now she needed to go explain herself to Naomi. Rose told him how sorry she was for keeping everything a secret all his life. She hugged him, told him that all of this was for his safety and wellbeing and that she only hoped one day he would truly understand, that he would grow to be a strong and healthy man with a family of his own. They cried together, and Willem told her that he understood, and wished she would have told him before.

Parking her car next to Naomi's in the driveway, she turned the ignition off, and faced Willem, "Now, let me go explain these things to Naomi, Son, alright? You stay here in the car. I'll leave the door open if you need me, okay?"

"Okay, Mom. Love you."

Rose's eyes filled with tears again, this time, proud tears for the well-mannered, heartfelt, young man she saw before her now, the son she had raised alone, with no one there to help and support her. "My son . . ." she said as she put her palm to his cheek. "I love you so much."

Approaching the house, Rose knocked, and when there was no answer, she opened the front door and stepped inside. While peaking her head out, she waved at Willem to show she was leaving the front door open if he needed her.

In the house, Rose found Naomi in her study, passed out; face down on the floor, naked. She ran to Naomi, calling her name aloud. When there was no response, Rose realized the situation, and checked Naomi's pulse. A slow beat, too slow. Her breathing was short and shallow. Rose ran back to her car and grabbed her portable nursing bag, telling Willem, "Stay here!" She ran back into the house, and in the kitchen she saw the glass Naomi had used. Rose took a quick moment to examine the remaining particles still in the bottom of the glass. Using a fingertip, she swiped up to the edge the grainy wine soaked flakes, and tasted it with the tip of her tongue. "Sleeping aides," she mumbled. She ran to Naomi and sat her up against a chaise she was lying near. Rose shook Naomi's shoulders. Not having any response, she slipped Naomi's arm over her shoulder, and brought her to a standing position. Rose slapped her gently on the cheek with her free hand, and called out, "Naomi!"

As close to walking as it could be called, Rose led her friend to the bathroom. Water had flooded out the door into the hallway. Rose sat Naomi on the side of the bathtub. Holding Naomi with one arm around her waist, she reached to turn the water off, and then pulled the drain cord. She swooped some of the now cold water in one hand and splashed it onto Naomi's face, calling out her name over and over again. Feeling that Naomi's pulse had slowed to a near stop, Rose grabbed from her bag an ope-hefren needle, and stabbed it squarely into Naomi's heart, having pierced through her chest plate; not an easy feat. Within a second, Naomi drew in a huge breath of air, and her eyes opened shockingly. She looked at the needle in her chest, and up to see Rose kneeling in front of her, soaking wet on her bathroom floor, eyes wide-filled with alarm. Naomi burst into silent tears as she cried out to her friend, Rose, sitting there in front of her, lips quivering, "I'm so sorry . . ."

"Oh-no, Naomi! I'm the one who is sorry . . ." Rose replied, and gently pulled the needle from Naomi's chest, and she dropped then to the floor next to her. They grabbed each other in an embrace and cried even more. A whispered laughter escaped them as they realized how soaking wet they were, and that Naomi was still buck naked.

Grabbing a towel, Rose wrapped it around Naomi's shoulders, and suggested they get her dressed, "Let's get you cleaned up, Sweetie." Running her finger through Naomi's curly copper colored hair, Rose smiled and told Naomi how very sorry she was for everything.

Naomi shook her head, grinning slightly, her eyes still immersed in tears, "It's all water under the bridge now, right?"

After a shower, Rose helped Naomi dress into an emerald colored loose fitting light sundress; it flowed nearly to the ground and reminded Rose of their childhood days in elementary school back in Nebraska. They ate whole wheat crackers and cream cheese in the kitchen with some warm tea and honey. Afterwards, they retreated to the porch deck to take in the evening air. The beautiful views of the mountains that erected high and wide, lined behind the river outside the house, and as they gazed onto the scenery in front of them, Naomi began to tell Rose more about the new explosions since they had talked on the phone that day she invited Rose to her Gallery Event. She told Rose that Jacob had been in a car accident and that he was very ill.

Rose interrupted in a patient manner, and told Naomi that she knew all of these things, that she had followed Naomi in the hospital. She told Naomi that she had gone to visit Jacob and found a man in his room. "He told the nurses he was Jacob's father, Naomi, but it wasn't Richard. I called out Richards's name, and the guy nearly knocked me over trying to run out of the room passed me. I think he . . ."

Their conversation was interrupted by a man's voice calling out from within the house, "Anyone home?"

Startled, Rose asked "Who's there?" She held a washcloth to Naomi's forehead as she stretched her neck and tried to peer her eyes over the back of Naomi's lawn chair to see into the house. They grabbed each other's hands when no one responded and fright took hold of them.

Ten seconds passed in slow motion, and as Rose started to stand to go and see who was in the house, Frank Calister emerged from the kitchen and onto the deck. He paused, gave a slight smile, and pointed his gun. He fired two shots. One hit Rose in the chest, and the other pierced Naomi's neck.

Satisfied he had severed a part of the ties to the project site, he stood over the bodies of Naomi Willem and Rose Carson, admiring his work and announced in a challenging way, "Next!"

Calister left the house and as he did so, he shut the front door behind him and proceeded down the long driveway to his car.

Willem Carson, still outside awaiting his mother's return, knew in his gut that something was wrong.

CHAPTER 20

SICK OF IT

Willem Carson, fourteen years old, feeling weak from just being released from the hospital; used to being sick, sick of being sick, pissed off about being sick—watched as his mom drove silently, only crying, until he finally asked her what was wrong, and where they were going. Usually after a hospital stay, Rose would be telling him everything would be okay, but this time she began to cry the moment they left the hospital. When Willem asked her about his dad, she told him everything, and about Naomi, her lifelong best friend. She told him his dad is sick and they would visit him tomorrow after Willem rested, but first they needed to make a stop. Rose explained she needed to explain things to Naomi, to tell her how sorry she was, and to try to make amends. She told Willem that after she talked with Naomi, she would introduce him to her.

They pulled up the driveway to Naomi and Jacob's house as Willem asked her, "This is where my dad lives?"

"Yes, Sweetie," touching his cheek, "Wait here."

"Okay, Mom. Love you," Willem told Rose, and she returned the gesture with a motherly smile and caress, "My son . . ." she said "I love you so much."

He watched his mom as she entered the house and left the front door open. He was used to her doing that. Rose being a nurse, and Willem an ill boy restricted to home care, he would often go with Rose to visit her patients. The ones that Willem could not go in the homes to visit because of their own illnesses or infections that he could not risk being exposed to, he would often wait in the car. Leaving the front door open became a habit they were both used to as this was Rose's way of telling Willem she wasn't far away if he needed her for anything. "All you have to do is yell out," she would tell Willem. She never shut any doors at their apartment either. "Just in case you need me," Rose would tell him. Always a bit annoyed, Willem knew his mother loved him deeply. His grandfather had died last year after Christmas, and the only family his mom had that ever came to visit was some cousins from Nebraska one time when he was a toddler. It had always been just him and his mom. He admired her for that, even at his young age, he knew she was the bravest person he would ever know.

Only a few minutes passed until Willem had fallen asleep in the car; wrapped up in a blanket, warm and cozy, exhausted from medicine treatments and his hospital stay. His dreams were always vivid. Often he would wake feeling as though he were still dreaming, and then he would wonder while awake that maybe he was dreaming, especially on the bad days from his chemotherapy treatments. Those days he especially liked to imagine that he was dreaming, and that he could wake from the pain, the shivers, all the violent vomiting, the high fevers, and dizzy spells at any given moment. Often he would pinch his arm just to make sure, of course to be followed by disappointment that he was, in fact, very much awake.

Suddenly feeling chilled, Willem opened his eyes and was startled by the sound of a car door shutting. He ducked down, afraid, but wasn't sure why. He climbed over the middle console to the backseat to peak his eyes slightly over the carpeted stereo cover behind the backseat head-rests. He saw a tall man standing by a car staring up at the house.

Willem ducked his head back down, grabbed his blanket from the front seat quickly, trying to be as quiet and motionless as he possibly could. He covered himself with the blanket in the backseat, hoping not to be seen. Pulling the blanket over his head, he slightly folded it in a way to allow his left eye to be exposed, enabling him to see out the side window above his feet as he lay as flat as he could on his back and side in the rear seat. Willem watched as this tall man passed by their car, and leaned forward enough to see the tall man enter the house. He closed the door behind him.

A few moments later he heard two long buzzing sounds echo through the valley air. He wondered what the noise was, and thought it sounded like his paintball air gun that his grandpa had given him as a present for their last Christmas before he passed away, or maybe it was a noise similar to the time that his mom let him have his ear pierced; that quick loud whisper of the ear-piercing-gun shooting an earring through his ear and clasping tight against his earlobe. Willem reached to feel his ear where only a slight lump remained from the skin that had grown over the once pierced hole, and felt sad about all the things in life he had to give up because of tests and CAT Scans he had to endure at the hospitals all of his life.

The noise echoed through the cold mountain air. Scared, Willem quickly slipped out of the car and ran towards the side of the house. His breath was short, and he quickly felt weak, so he hid on the side of the house, crouching down as small as he could make himself towards the ground, holding his hand hard against his mouth so he wouldn't cough out loud. He watched as the tall man walked out from the house, down the driveway to his car and quickly drove away. Willem saw his license plate, BWT-079. He remembered his mom always telling him if he were ever in any kind of trouble with a stranger, to get a good look at the person's clothes and face, to look at their car; the type of car, the color, and the license plate. This man was driving a new Mercedes-Benz, it was a two door, it was bright silver, and he was very tall, older like his grandpa was.

Willem Carson walked to the front door but it was locked. Nobody answered when he rang the doorbell. Scared even more now, he ran as fast as he could around to the side of the house again, this time farther back, stopping every few feet to catch his breath. When he reached the backyard, he climbed over the fence and hurried up the steps.

His mom, Rose, was lying flat on her back on the ground of the deck. Her eyes were wide open, and when he walked over to her, she seemed to be staring right at him. Her upper body was covered in blood.

"Mom!" Willem screamed.

When she did not respond, he froze in the moment. Shock quickly set in. He couldn't touch her, he couldn't move, he didn't feel like he could do anything except cry out to her, "Mom! Mom, no, please wake up! Mom, wake up . . ." he whispered in horror.

Only a moment later, Willem fell then to his knees, tears streaming down his cheeks, and he felt the shortness in his breath take over his focus. Short breaths of air, in and out, raspy. He reached in his pocket for his inhaler and took a quick puff of the inhalant. His heart was racing fast, and his focus was wild eyed, glancing all around him though he did not know what he was looking for.

His eyes shifted when he noticed a motion beside his mother. A woman was lying there on a long-lawn chair. She was sprawled out, legs hanging off the chair, her arms were dangling beside her, and blood was dripping from her neck. His eyes shifted to her hand. Drops of blood were falling from her fingertips one at a time, like a teardrop but dark, a crayon's deep brick red. She was slowly moving her hand up and down, motioning for him to come closer.

Wiping the tears from his face, Willem crawled on his knees closer and whispered to the bloodied woman, "Are you Naomi . . . my dad's wife?"

Touching his face with her fingertips, she responded softly, "Yes, Will . . . now call 911."

CHAPTER 21

TALL MAN

When the police arrived at Jacob and Naomi Willem's house, Willem Carson was still kneeling next to his mother, Rose, but this time he knelt amongst the bloodied scene in between her and Naomi, still lying on that long lawn chair. The police came in without a warning, and suddenly Willem found himself swarmed with men in blue uniforms, their guns in hand, and standing over him. One woman police officer took Willem by the arm and pulled him aside, out of sight of Rose and Naomi's bodies, into the kitchen.

The emergency medical teams arrived shortly after, with the ambulance and a fire response truck. While a detective questioned Willem on the details of what he had seen there, Willem heard an EMT announce "Dead on arrival." They were talking about his mom; he knew that, after all Naomi was still talking and breathing.

As police questioned Willem Carson, investigators began marking off areas with yellow do-not-cross tape, and one began to outline Rose Carson's body. Willem was standing in the kitchen and watched as they traced a chalk outline around his mother's body lying still and dead on the hardwood deck ground outside. Shock written across Willem's face, the woman police officer noticed his view of the bodies, and quickly escorted him out the front door towards her police car. She pulled disinfectant wipes from the EMT's supply in the ambulance and returned to Willem. She proceeded to gently clean the blood off of his cheek where Naomi had ran her fingers, and the blood from his neck and arms when he had leaned over his mom's bloodied dead body and crawled across her to Naomi's side before calling 911.

Eventually another detective came over to the squad car and began questioning Willem more in detail. The woman officer told the detective that the boy was outside in the car of the victim . . . his mother . . . when he heard shots go off from inside the house, but that he ran to the back of the house afterward.

Detective Charlie Moore knelt down on one knee to the ground in front of Willem where he had been seated in the passenger seat of the police officer's squad car. Detective Moore asked Willem if he was okay, and Willem nodded that he was. The detective proceeded to question Willem, "Son, did you see who did this to your mom and to Mrs. Willem?"

"Yes, Sir," Willem responded quietly.

"Do you know this person who did this, Son? Have you ever seen this person before today?"

"No, Sir, I don't know who he is."

"So, it was a man that shot your momma, Will?"

He nodded again and replied, "Yes, Sir, a tall man did it." Willem began to cry silently. He was scared and wished he had done something other than hide in the car.

Detective Moore placed a hand on Willem's shoulder, "I'm sorry, Son. This will be over in just a minute, alright? I only need you to answer a few more questions, and then Police Officer Julie Harris here will take you home. Do you know if your dad is home, Son? Do you know your address?"

"I don't have a da . . . well; actually, he's in the hospital. My Mom brought me here to meet his wife, Naomi."

"Naomi Willem is your step-mother then? Is your father Jacob Willem?"

"Yes, Sir. My mom was going to take me to meet him tomorrow . . ." and Willem began to cry again, knowing that moment that he would never see his mom again, never see her leave the door open for his safety, and never again hear her tell him that everything would be okay or that she loved him. He couldn't contain himself, nor was there a thought that he was supposed to do so. He lunged toward Officer Harris, innocent, and vulnerable to this scary world he was suddenly exposed to, much scarier, he knew, than the ill-lived life he had known too well thus far; he fell into her arms. Officer Julie Harris hugged him tight, rocking him slowly, and she turned to Detective Moore and suggested they finish later.

"Only a couple more questions," Moore retorted.

Willem wiped his tears and tried to sit up straight to talk to the Detective again.

"Will, Willem . . . Son. Did you see this tall man's face? Can you tell me what he looked like?"

Sniffling, Willem tried to remember anything about the man other than that he was tall. "He was white, but he looked really tan, and he was wearing a dark suit. He looked about your age, Sir. I saw the car he was driving!"

"Good, Son, now what was it? Do you know what kind of car it was?"

"Yes, Sir. It was a Mercedes-Benz, a new one. It was bright silver, and only had two doors."

"Good boy, Will. Thank you. Is there anything else you can tell me?"

"Well, I saw his license plate. Will that help?" Willem asked.

Detective Moore gave him a big smile, patted his shoulder once more, and told him that would be a big help, and Willem told him.

"Thank you, Son. Officer Harris, Darlin', will you see that this young man is taken care of properly?"

"Yes, Sir, Detective," Harris replied half annoyed; she never liked Charlie Moore much. They had gone to high school together and were in the same police academy. They graduated and were both hired into the same division. Charlie received a promotion to detective soon after that, and he always treated Julie like she didn't belong, often referring to her as "Darlin'," which she despised. Having to take orders from him reached beneath her skin quick, deep, and sharp, but she complied for the sake of young Willem Carson.

"Ma'am, do you think I can stay here with Mrs. Naomi?" Willem asked Officer Harris.

"Will, the EMTs are going to have to take her to the hospital to make sure she'll be alright. She has lost a lot of blood, and that can make a person really weak." Harris explained.

"But my mom was going to take me there to see my dad tomorrow, and if Mrs. Naomi is going to be there, can't I just be with her?"

"Let me see what I can do, alright? Do you know what hospital your dad is at?"

"Yes, Ma'am, he's at St. Jude's downtown. That's where my mom always takes me when I have a bad reaction from my treatments."

"What treatments, Will?"

"I have cancer. Sometimes the Chemo makes me really sick."

A moment of silence passed as Officer Harris looked at Willem, really looked at him for the first time, and she could see now that he was in deed an ill boy. She stood and told him to wait in her squad car. "Now, don't you touch anything," she told Willem with a friendly smile, "and I'll be right back."

Julie Harris walked to the ambulance where EMTs were already lifting Naomi on a stretcher into the back of the ambulance. She told the EMTs crew leader about Willem Carson having cancer and that the dead body on the deck was his mom. She explained that this woman they were lifting into the ambulance, Naomi Willem, was his step-mother, and the boy's dad was already in the hospital at St. Jude's. "Is there any chance you can take Naomi Willem there, and I'll follow with the boy?" Harris asked. "I know it's out of our jurisdiction, but you'd be doing me a huge favor."

"The victim is stable enough. We should be able to get cleared for that," the EMT complied, and away they all left to St. Jude's in downtown Ballard.

Nearly an hour later, they pulled into the hospital at the emergency room entrance and raced Naomi inside to be treated. Officer Harris escorted Willem Carson inside, and found out his father, Jacob Willem, was quarantined and not able to take visitors. Officer Harris explained to the nurse that Willem Carson was his son, his mother was just killed less than two hours ago, and his step-mother, Naomi Willem, was just taken into E.R. for surgery because of a gunshot wound to the neck. She asked if they had emergency contacts listed in their system, and the nurse informed her that the emergency contact for Naomi Willem was one Irene O'Brien.

Officer Harris called Naomi's mother, Irene, and informed her of the situation. Irene, shocked to hear about Jacob's son, Willem Carson, did not lead on to the matter of her surprise and told Officer Harris she would be there as soon as possible.

Forty five minutes later, Irene O'Brien walked through the emergency room sliding glass doors, and saw a female officer standing with a young boy, tall, and thin. She approached them, shook the officer's hand and thanked her.

Officer Harris handed her a business card and asked that they call her if they needed anything. She hugged Willem one last time and turned to leave the hospital. In her squad car, she radioed Detective Moore. "Charlie, I took the boy to St. Jude's downtown with the female victim, Naomi Willem. Her mother, Irene O'Brien is here with the boy. I thought you should know that Jacob Willem is also here in emergency. Isn't he the one we had a call about the other day from that Borgam guy? Crione Agency, I think it was. Apparently there was a car accident, but there's something else wrong with the guy. Maybe check the accident reports from the last few days to get the details. My shift's over, so I'm headed home unless you need me for anything."

"Nice work, Darlin'. I'll come check it out after a while."

"Right. You do that, Charlie. And, it's Officer Harris, or Julie, like I've told you a million times before."

"Right on, Darlin'. I'll keep that in mind . . ."

Watching Officer Harris leave, Irene O'Brien turned to Willem to introduce herself. "Hello there, Willem. My name is Irene. I'm your grandma!"

Willem looked at Irene, wide eyed, exhausted, and overwhelmed; he fell into her arms. They stood in that embrace until their arms went numb. "We're going to wait here until we can see Naomi, would that be alright?"

"Yes, Ma'am, umm, I mean, Grandma," Willem smiled.

They sat and talked, and Willem told his new grandma everything he had told the officers. He grew tired quickly throughout the conversation, cried off and on, and so Irene comforted him with her arm hugging tight across his shoulders as they sat next to each other, close, keeping one another warm in that cold, sterile, overcrowded, emergency waiting room; and so they waited.

CHAPTER 22

BLOODY HANDS

Detective Charlie Moore and Officer Julie Harris left the station to drive to St. Jude's hospital the following morning. Moore had already searched the license plate number that young Willem Carson had provided them the day before. He had discovered that the 2006 Mercedes-Benz was registered to one, Thomas D. Krindle of Crione Agency. Tommy Krindle was now their top suspect. They called Krindle's office but were unable to locate him at Crione Agency.

Moore decided now was a good time to make the Willems' talk, as they knew Jacob Willem worked for Crione Agency because Clint Borgam had called the station searching for him the other night. Officer Harris just happened to be the one Borgam had spoken with.

Detective Moore yelled at Officer Harris, "Hey Darlin', we have a lead. Let's go talk to your girl."

Surprised Moore asked her to assist, she did not argue this time, and ignored Charlie calling her "Darlin'" once again.

On the way out, Harris suggested they question Tami Krindle first. Moore agreed. They called in a locate for Krindle's address, and thirty minutes later they were knocking on the front door.

A young woman answered the door, dressed in her lavender maid's dress and white apron wrapped neatly around her waist, the top portion tied behind her neck. She was a pretty thing, Moore thought. "Hello, Miss. Detective Moore and Officer Harris here. Are Tommy and Tami Krindle about?"

The young housekeeper responded that Mr. Krindle was not available, but she would call for Mrs. Krindle, and escorted them inside to the Formal Reading Room. The young lady offered them something to drink and asked that they sit until she returned. The officers declined the beverage and stayed standing as the young woman left the room.

A few moments later, Tami Krindle appeared. "Good morning. Can I help you?"

"Yes, hello, Mrs. Krindle . . . can I call you Tami?" Moore spoke first.

"That's fine. What is this about?"

Moore continued; he introduced himself as well as Officer Julie Harris. He asked Tami Krindle where they could find her husband, and when she expected him to be home.

"My goodness! I'm sorry, Officers, but I really don't know. He hasn't been home in nearly a week, and I haven't heard a single peep from him."

"Is that normal behavior of your husband?" Harris asked.

"Well, yes, I suppose it is. He's a busy man, and I'm a busy woman. I have this big house to tend to and our four young boys to look after. Tommy's away often on work trips."

"And he doesn't call first? Mrs. Krindle, have the two of you had any kind of argument recently?" Harris continued with her inquiries.

"Well, no, we haven't. What is this about? You still haven't answered my question." Tami snapped back commandingly.

"Tami," Moore chimed in, "your husband is a suspect in the murder of Rose Carson, attempted murder of Naomi Willem, and conspiracy to cover up multiple allegations involving his work with Crione Agency. We have a warrant for his arrest, and it is dire that we speak with him, to clear these charges, you see."

Tami thought quietly for a long period of time, looking the officers up and down, judging their intentions, and intrusion at her home. Finally she responded, "Detective Moore. Officer . . . Harris, is it?" Not waiting for a response, Tami continued, "I do not know where my husband is. I filed a missing person report for him four days ago. You don't have to be a detective to recognize an old and tired marriage. We don't keep tabs on each other, and Tommy's reputation is not a secret. He likes his young women, but he is dedicated to his work, and to Crione Agency. You need to speak with Clint Borgam, and Frank Calister. I really don't know any details on their work there though. They all work closely with Naomi Willem's husband, Jacob, as well, whom I have already spoken with myself just the other day. I'll tell you one thing, that woman is not stable. If you ask me, you are looking for the wrong person, and—"

Detective Moore interrupted. "Are you suggesting that Jacob Willem is involved in this murder case . . ." clearing his throat, "these allegations? Are you saying you believe Jacob Willem is behind the murder of Miss Rose Carson, and attempted murder of his own wife?"

"That is exactly what I am saying."

"Is your husband a tall man, Tami?"

She laughed, "You obviously don't know my husband. Why don't you do your job and read the missing person report? You'll see that he is indeed not a tall man. Now, if you'll excuse me, I have work to do."

"Just one more thing, Mrs. Krindle," Harris spoke up. "There was a witness at the Willems' house last night. Our witness has identified the suspect, and saw his car. That car is a silver Mercedes-Benz, Mrs. Krindle. It is registered under your husband's name."

Unfazed, lips puckered to a bitter smirk, Tami let out a sinister laugh and responded, "Young lady, all of Crione's employee vehicles are registered to my husband."

"I see," Harris said, nodding her head up and down. "Well, we thank you for your time, Ma'am."

Harris and Moore turned to walk to the door, and with one foot out the door, Julie Harris turned back to face Tami Krindle, reaching her hand inside past the door frame and held out their business card, "I almost forgot. Here's our card. Call if you think of anything else, would you?"

"Of course," Tami replied, hand on the doorknob, anxious for them to leave.

"Ooh, and Tami, what did you say your husband does there at Crione Agency?" Detective Moore asked nonchalantly.

"He's an engineer," Tami answered and bid them goodbye, shutting the door briskly behind them.

Julie looked at Charlie, "Just an engineer, huh? Right. Every engineer registers company vehicles to employees under their own name," she retorted in a sarcastic tone. "She's a piece of work, that one."

"Right?" Charlie responded. "And, another thing, he doesn't fit the description Willem Carson gave us either. If Krindle is a short man, then who the hell is this tall man?"

"She mentioned Clint Borgam's name. He's the one I told you about that called in looking for Jacob Willem. Maybe we should check him out, too," Julie suggested.

"Right. And the other fellow she told us. What was it . . . ?" Charlie responded.

Flipping through her notepad, Julie responded. "Frank Calister."

Awhile later, Detective Moore and Officer Harris arrived at St. Jude's where both Jacob and Naomi Willem were hospitalized.

They first met with medical staff and were briefed on the conditions and status of the Willems'. They were informed by both of the Willems' doctor's that they had determined there had been some form of nuclear exposure at Crione Agency. Diagnosis was still pending for Jacob, but in the meantime, they were treating his injuries from the car accident he'd had, informing the officers that his condition was severe; several broken bones and a collapsed lung. Jacob Willem would remain quarantined until a diagnosis was determined. They would not be allowed in his room at this time. Continuing the discussion regarding Naomi Willem, the other doctor explained she was doing much better after surgery; they had stitched the wound from the bullet that pierced through her neck. Naomi would most likely be released sometime that evening after her blood levels were stabilized.

Police visited with Naomi Willem after she woke from resting after surgery that prior night. They informed Naomi that her husband, Jacob Willem, is a suspect for the allegations made about Crione Agency. Harris and Moore explained that they needed to question him about his involvement with the shootings at Naomi's home last night.

Shaking her head, Naomi said aloud, "That's ridiculous! Where in the world did you get that absurd idea? Jacob wouldn't hurt a fly, much less Rose, and especially not me! I'm his wife for crying-out-loud."

Office Harris responded, "Don't you worry too much, Mrs. Willem. Your husband is only a suspect at this time. We just need to talk with him when he's stabilized. You know how following protocol goes, right? In the meantime, it looks like we're after Tommy Krindle. The license plate that your step-son, Willem, saw showed that the perpetrator's vehicle is registered under Krindle's name."

"What can you tell us about Crione Agency?" Detective Moore asked.

"This is all insane. I really don't know much about the agency except that they are all engineers, something to do with science and . . . well, I guess I really just don't know. Jacob doesn't talk about his work much . . ." Feeling weak Naomi continued, "I'm not feeling very clear headed right now. Do you think we can do this another time?"

"Of course," Harris responded.

"But the sooner we get your statement, Mrs. Willem, the sooner we can track down your killer," Moore chimed in.

"I really don't have much of a statement to make. I didn't see anyone. We only heard a man's voice asking if anyone was home and the next thing I knew, Rose was standing next to me, and we were both shot!" Naomi responded. "My step-son came to the deck a few minutes later, and I asked him to call 911."

"Alright, well, thank you, Mrs. Willem. We'll be in touch. Here's our card. Make sure you call us if you think of anything else!"

That evening, Naomi's status stabilized and she was allowed to go home. She thought to herself that no one needed to know about her taking those pills. She laid there on her hospital bed in the recovery room, and thought about her friend Rose saving her life, and she cried a few minutes until she could gain her composure. She wasn't sure, after all of this, if she was ready to face Jacob. They had so much to talk about but she knew he would be in no condition to do so. After her nurse confirmed that she would be able to visit with him, she decided to see Jacob anyway, for a brief moment.

While visiting, he was not alert long enough for her to tell him much. She managed to inform him about Rose and her being shot and that he has a son named Willem; "He's fourteen. He has cancer, Jacob, but is getting better. He saw the man that did this to us," she explained. Naomi asked Jacob if he knew about any of this, if he knew that he had a son. Jacob was too weak, thus unable to speak much, but he could hear, and he listened intently to every word Naomi spoke. He shook his head as to say no, he did not know about any of this. He did not know he had a son!

Naomi also told Jacob about the detectives questioning her about Crione Agency, and that Tommy Krindle was the main suspect. She paused momentarily while Jacob faded consciousness. "Jacob, you're a suspect, too. These detectives will be coming to question you."

Jacob managed to speak slowly now, and told her about Clint Borgam being in his room, and that he had tried to kill him. "I know about that," Naomi responded. "Rose . . . she had come to see you. She saw Borgam, Jacob . . . And now she's dead, and they tried to kill me, too. Police think you might be involved somehow!"

"Naomi . . . my joy, please tell me that you know better than to think that." Pausing in between words, his breaths short and shallow, he continued on, telling her not to say anything to the police. "Let me answer their questions, Naomi. Be as elusive as you can."

"Well, I don't seem to really know anything about you these days anyhow, do I? And I surely do not know what you do for Crione Agency. Do I, Jacob? So, I can imagine that my being *ELUSIVE* won't be difficult." Frustrated, still hurt, and scared, Naomi stood to leave.

She looked back at her husband lying there in that hospital bed, hooked up to numerous machines, his body parts in casts, all the tubes dripping whatever kind of fluids into his veins, she did not know, and she felt sorry for him. She felt sorry for them, their lives, and their marriage, for not being able to have a child of their own, and for everything that had gone wrong.

"I do love you, Jacob. I always will. We'll get through all of this, won't we?"

"I only hope so, Naomi. I love you more than life . . . . you're my joy," Jacob whispered, tears forming in his eyes, and he began to feel faint again. He closed his eyes and quickly drifted off, having fallen asleep while she still stood there watching him.

Naomi walked back to his bedside, and used the bedside hospital phone to call for a taxi-cab.

An hour and a half later, she was home, where she found her mother, Irene, there with her step-son, Willem. They had dinner together that Irene had cooked, and after settling Willem down for bed in their spare guest bedroom, she and her mother talked for hours, catching up on each other's lives, and all the mess that had occurred in recent days. Naomi wasn't sure why, but she didn't tell her mom that Jacob knew about Willem yet. Through all the discussion, Irene changed the subject, trying to lighten the mood, and asked Naomi about her painting. Reflecting on her last piece she had accomplished the night before, after taking those pills, Naomi realized she would need to reschedule her gallery event. Waving at the air, "There's just too much going on, Mom. I'll tell you all about it later. I have work to do," and Naomi walked to her study to reschedule the Gallery Event.

CHAPTER 23

LIKE FATHER LIKE SON

That night Jacob took a turn for the worse. His veins had grown black as night, he had a 104 fever, his skin texture changed to a rough sand paper like appearance in patches across face, chest, and legs, and his entire exterior body color had changed to an intense red. He was blistering. He itched everywhere but the pain was too extreme to even touch his own skin. His hair was thinning quickly, clumps were falling out. He was experiencing uncontrollable shakes and seizures, night tremors when sleeping caused disorientation when he would wake and he couldn't stay alert for long periods at a time. His breath was weak and his head was piercing with pain. He was experiencing heavy diarrhea and would often soil himself. Nausea was a constant presence though vomiting had subsided which nurses were relieved of because of the way they had him secured him in bed for his broken bones, he would've choked on his own reflux.

Doctors determined he had a severe form of *Acute Radiation Syndrome and Jacob would have to fight to live. They began administering treatments for Radiation Toxicity, and treatments with the use of antibiotics, other blood products for colon stimulating factors, and considered stem cell transplants through therapeutic interventions. They administered antimicrobials for infections, and determined his illness had something to do with the *absolute lymphocyte test count resulting at nearly 0.35Gy. This determined Jacob's radiation exposure through inhalation of poisons and particles in the air that can only occur after months of exposure to ionizing radiation.

They explained to him that most patients died within 48 hours of this exposure, and asked Jacob if he had been exposed to any explosions or nuclear leaks with his job. He managed to tell them about the punctured holding tanks at Crione Agency, but never mentioned his involvement at the actual project site. He had enough wits about him to keep secret most details that tied him to the accidents on that mountain.

Jacob had developed severe gastrointestinal infections and internal bleeding, a Hematopoietic Syndrome caused from a drop in white blood cells that were caused from his radiation exposure. Afraid of the neurological effects to soon follow, doctors started new antimicrobial and oxygen treatments. They told him the only way to cure his symptoms was to avoid more exposure, and warned Jacob never to return to Crione Agency, or the area these nuclear vessels were stored. Doctors asked his permission to inform his wife and then called Naomi with the news.

Still too weak to talk to police, Jacob laid in his bed, scared for his life, scared he would not be able to see his wife again, scared she would never truly understand, scared he would never get to meet his son . . . "I have a son," he whispered aloud.

Jacob laid in that hospital room, his leg in a cast, pins holding his upper body in place due to his broken collar bone, his arm also in a cast, bandages on his head and chest. He was still hooked to a lung machine and heart monitor. IV drips were attached so saline could clear his veins. He had other tubes running in and out of him for the administering of pain medicines, antibiotics for inflammation, and the antimicrobial infection fluid drip for his colon. His mouth and nose had attached over them an oxygen mask that felt like it covered his entire face.

Jacob was in and out of consciousness, and his mind full of too many thoughts. He feared when police would come to question him, and how he would prove his involvement was a part of his job, that Clint Borgam and Frank Calister were in charge, and that he really did not know much about Tommy Krindle. The truth of the matter was that Jacob's hands were just as bloody as any of theirs were. He helped burn those bodies in the containment room, and load the rest onto the trucks to take them away. The bodies of his crew still lay under the pile of debris passed the tunnel entrance and into the holding tank room. There was no evidence though that led Jacob to the site. All of his work was designed to appear as though he worked solely out of the development center at Crione Agency. What about his son, he thought again. Would he ever meet him? Was he going to die right here in this hospital room? He thought about the night he left the house feeling ill and angry with Naomi . . . Why was he driving to Rose's apartment? He wondered in worry about all of these things.

Feeling disillusioned, imagining his conversation with Krindle at the Glacier Point Peak project site, he let out a scream, "I was only doing my job, damn it." In his sleep, Jacob's mumbling grew louder with each moan. "Damn you, Borgam!" Jacob yelled aloud from his sleep.

Detective Moore and Officer Harris were standing outside Jacob's room and heard him yell out Borgam's name. The nurse was briefing them on Jacob Willem's status and diagnoses, as well as the treatments administered. "Hopefully, we'll be able to get him stabilized. He has made it longer than anticipated. He must be a fighter!" she told them. "And then he'll be moved to his own room upstairs near the Card iatric unit. You'll be able to talk with him there all you'd like," the nurse explained. "Right now, I'm afraid he's too weak, and disillusioned from the all the medicines. Wouldn't do ya' any good to talk to him now, I'm afraid."

Frustrated they could not question him yet, the officers left to drive back to headquarters.

"Who and where is Borgam? And, Calister, damn it. And what about Tommy Krindle? We need some flipping' answers already!" Detective Moore shouted aloud to Officer Harris.

They issued a warrant for the arrest of Tommy Krindle, and obtained a search warrant for Crione Agency. Discovering that they were all still missing, and with Jacob in the hospital all this time, they had nothing to piece together the clues. Clues only being names at this point, and speculations from bystanders about the goings on within Crione Agency. They needed answers. The needed details, anything to explain what exactly linked Rose Carson's murder to Crione Agency, and the profession of all those so called engineers.

The late night turned quickly to dawn the following day, and Detective Moore and Officer Harris headed to Crione Agency with their search warrant in pocket. They searched Frank Calister, Clint Borgam, and Jacob Willem's offices. They couldn't find an office for Tommy Krindle, which they thought was incredibly strange. In Calister's office were memos and dispatcher logs all addressed to Mr. Willem, all sent from either Borgam or Calister. There were no details to explain anything in concrete. Just orders regarding when and where to be for something called the * "Nuclear Club Project." Its outline showed the project site location on Glacier Point Peak, and there were blueprints and other engineering documents in Jacob's office outlining designs for some sort of safety tanks. The documents in Calister's folder were listed "Top Secret," and showed only that "Subject is to disclose nuclear vessels in a sealed container to be stored below ground for Undisclosed Recipient." The folders for this project were stamped in large red bold letters, "FUNDED."

There was nothing linking anything to anyone in particular except call logs and memos with Mr. Willem's name mentioned. Finding themselves beyond frustrated, they tore a little deeper into filing cabinets, and found that Jacob Willem was in charge of the "Nuclear Club Project's Safety Team." He was training people for safety precautions in some development center on site at Crione Agency, and there were blueprints for these safety tanks they had invented and built, all signed by Jacob Willem. Nothing linked him so far to the allegations made at Glacier Point Peak Pass. There were, however, detailed documentation for the planning and storing of nuclear weaponry for an unknown recipient, all addressed to Frank Calister.

Officer Harris headed back to Calister's office and found a piece of scribbled on paper that had been crumbled up and thrown away in a trashcan beside his desk. It was a hand written itinerary, listing reminders for a private jet flight booked to Omaha, NE, and then to France with Mr. Willem. There were no exact flight destinations, dates, or times noted, but the officer and Detective Moore felt they finally had something to link Jacob Willem to the allegations of conspiracy and murder that Crione Agency was now facing.

"We have to find Frank Calister!" Moore grumbled to Harris.

"Yep, and who and where is Krindle and this Borgam guy?" She responded.

"We'll head to Jacob Willem's place on our way out. If Jacob can't talk, we'll make your girl tell us something!"

"You mean Naomi Willem? You really think she knows anything?"

"At this point, it can't hurt to try, now can it, Darlin'?"

Rolling her eyes at Charlie Moore, Julie Harris, grabbed the evidence up that they had accumulated at Crione Agency, and placed it all in a large cardboard filing box. "Well, let's do this, Boss-man!"

CHAPTER 24

LOW DOWN

Naomi was at home, having finished fixing breakfast for Willem, she sat with him at the kitchen table as she watched him eat. They spoke simply and seldom with one another; Willem still holding all of his emotions inside. Naomi sliced a pear for herself and felt warmth inside of her as she shared this simple moment with her new found son, a hole missing in her life suddenly filled in. "We'll find out who did this to your mom, Willem, I swear we will." Naomi finally spoke, breaking the ice.

She stood to prepare his daily regimen of medicines, and told him, "We'll go get more of your things today from your apartment if you'd like, Willem. Would you like that?"

"Sure," he responded.

Naomi walked to the sink and placed their plates and her knife gently at the bottom, rinsing them off with the nozzle spray hose. She looked at Willem and gave him a soft smile. When he returned the gesture, Naomi turned away towards her study.

"Naomi?" Willem called out to her.

"Yes?"

"Umm, thanks."

"Would you like this to be your home, Willem? Your dad and I want you here, and your mom's cousins in Nebraska agree that this is your decision. I know how hard all of this must be, Son, and well, I just want you to know that we love you, and we are going to get through all of this . . . Together, okay?"

Willem ran to Naomi, and they stood embraced in a long hug; One that they both had been longing for, but had not known how to cross that line to. Naomi held him in a tight hug as her chin rested on his hair. With his cheek against her chest-plate, she swayed him slowly back and forth, gently side to side. Willem began to cry quietly, cold tears running down his cheeks. So much despair and heartache for a young man, so much loss, so much gained, and he felt conflicted inside. He missed his mom, and still hadn't met his dad. He asked Naomi, "Can I meet him soon? When will my dad come home?"

"Soon, Sweetie, soon."

In her study, Naomi had finished the details for floral arrangements and phone calls to Rose's friends that Willem had told her about. The funeral would take place in a couple days. All she knew at first was how to get a hold of some of Rose's cousins in Nebraska. They notified Rose's mother and step-father in Omaha that Rose had grown estranged from over the years, and made all the arrangements for the services near Ballard in Washington. The family was going to fly out, and some would even stay with Naomi at their house near Darrington. She knew Jacob would not be able to be there, so she asked her mother, Irene, to stay as well.

Sitting back in her chair, missing her friend, Rose, regretting all the years that had passed before reuniting, her thoughts flooded with all of their childhood memories together, and in Cambridge. Naomi's thoughts drifted to Willem, being able to provide for him; financially, spiritually, physically, mentally—his medical cares, being able to give him the love and support he needed, even more now.

She daydreamed about the times they would all have together as a family once Jacob was out of the hospital and back home with them; picnics, holidays, family functions, shopping, mall trips, movies nights, games, silly songs during road trips, and all the conversations they would have together, Mother and Son.

Naomi began to worry about Jacob, and everything the doctor had told her on the phone the day before. She had a feeling deep down within her that Jacob was more involved in all of this mess with Crione Agency than he'd ever led on. Why didn't he trust her? Why all of the lies? To protect her, she wondered. To protect his son. Had he known about Willem and lied about that as well? Did Rose ever tell him the truth? She thought back to when she was released from the hospital and their conversation, as one sided as it was, that Jacob had nodded that he knew nothing about Willem. Rose must have never told Jacob either, Naomi concluded.

Worry focused again on all the explosions, and Borgam never having called her back. She wondered how Borgam found Jacob in the hospital and the fact that the man tried to kill him! "What the hell is going on?" she said aloud to herself.

Still early morning, Naomi heard a knock on the front door, disrupting her meditation time with her thoughts. Willem, in the casual family room by the kitchen, slid down low on the couch as he watched Naomi approach the door and ask, "Who is it?"

"Police."

Willem heard them say they had a few questions. It was Detective Moore and Officer Harris. He recognized them but was feeling shy and withdrawn after all that had occurred. He really did not want to talk to them again, to anyone for that matter. All Willem really wanted right then was to meet his dad, Jacob, for the first time in his life, and for his mom to be alive. He liked his new grandma, Irene, and loved his new step-mom, but felt nearly guilty for loving her so soon. Would his mom be okay with that, he wondered. He decided then that he would call Naomi by her name, for now anyway.

Naomi welcomed the Detective and Officer inside and walked them to living room.

They asked her about Crione Agency, what they (the company) did there, what was Jacob's role there, and so on. Naomi explained that she wasn't exactly sure. The only thing she really knew was what Crione stood for; the Criminal Response agency for Interrogation and Nuclear Engineering. Naomi explained that Jacob never talked about his work but that he was an engineer, and that was all she really knew.

Continuing with their questioning, they asked her about Tommy Krindle again, and how to find him and said that Tami Krindle mentioned Naomi's name a couple of days ago. They asked her about Clint Borgam, and Frank Calister.

Naomi scurried to find Tommy Krindle's business card she had found in Jacob's desk, and handed it to Officer Harris to see. She explained that she had called them but Tami Krindle was the only one home, and she explained Tami had seemed bitter and snappy on the phone. She had told Naomi that Jacob was useless. Naomi continued and told the police how Tami had also mentioned that Tommy hadn't been home for several days. She didn't know where he was except to speculate that he may have been off with another woman.

Naomi explained that she had met Frank Calister once, at a dinner function but that was almost ten years ago. They had barely spoken other than an introduction. She knew Clint Borgam only briefly, explaining that he was Jacob's immediate boss. She'd seen him several times over the years when she would surprise Jacob at work with lunch.

She hadn't done that in nearly four years though, she realized, and told the Officer and Detective that she hadn't even seen Borgam since that time four years ago. She told them about her phone call with Borgam though, only a few days ago, "Just before I had called the Krindles, and I had called Borgam to ask about Jacob because he was late. Borgam didn't know where to find Jacob either but said that he would find out and call me. I never heard back from him."

Officer Harris asked, "Did you know, Mrs. Willem, before being shot that your husband, Jacob, was in the hospital?

Naomi explained her step-son was ill and that she had gone to the hospital downtown to meet her friend, Rose Carson and to visit with her step-son. Naomi told them that when she left, she heard Jacob's voice in the E.R. and that was how she found out he was even in the hospital. That was why he hadn't been home yet and no one seemed to know where he was. "He was in a horrible car crash," she told them, "And must have been on his way to visit his son." Naomi knew she was lying and wasn't sure why except that their personal lives were none of the officers' business, she thought, and then she remembered Jacob telling her to be elusive.

"What time did you talk to Borgam?" Detective Moore inquired.

Shaking her head slowly, side to side, lips puckered a bit while thinking, Naomi responded, "I don't know. It was late."

"How late, Naomi?"

"Maybe ten or so? I really don't know. Like I said, it was late."

A silence; awkwardness took over the conversation, and Naomi felt like the police officers were staring straight through her for some reason. Suddenly feeling uneasy and frustrated, Naomi's palms began to sweat.

Detective Moore interrupted the silence and asked, "Does Mr. Willem always work late hours, Naomi?"

There was a long pause before she answered. "No, he doesn't. There was an emergency. But he got sick and stayed home that day." She lied again, telling herself they didn't need to know that they had been fighting. They didn't need to know that Jacob was actually gone for two nights in a row and only had time enough to briefly come home, which was when they fought.

"Jacob started feeling better that evening though," Naomi continued, "and said he needed to get some work done. So he left. He went to his office, and was only going to be gone a few hours. When he wasn't home by ten, I called Borgam." She paused, staring back at the officers sitting in her living room, looking at them inquisitively and asked, "Is my husband in some kind of danger?"

The Detective responded, "What kind of danger?"

"I don't know. I guess I'm just not used to police knocking on my door first thing in the morning and questioning me about my husband's work, and I am certainly not accustomed to being shot at! For crying out loud, I just lost my best friend!" Shaking her head in disgust toward their inconsideration, Naomi continued, "I think I've answered enough of your questions. Now, please leave," and she stood up and began walking to the front door, hoping they would mirror her actions.

Detective Moore and Officer Harris sat for a moment, and gave each other a quick glance. They stood as well, and thanked Naomi for her time. They expressed their condolences for Rose Carson, and handed her their business card once again. Leaving, Officer Harris turned back to say, "We'll be in touch, Mrs. Willem. We still need to speak with your husband."

Naomi's mind was swirling. Her mother, Irene, was in the other room with Willem, eavesdropping the entire time and walked into the front living room where Naomi stood after the officers left.

Naomi plopped down into her comfy chair by their bay window, and sunk low down into the soft thick cushions as far as she could; wanting to disappear in it. She cried in a quiet whisper, speaking out loud, this time knowing she was not alone, "All this danger, people are missing . . . and dead. Rose has been murdered. Someone tried to kill me. I haven't even told you about Jacob! Someone tried to kill him, too . . . In his hospital bed for Pete's sake! And his accident, and his illness . . . These crazy explosions in the mountain," pointing towards the back of the house where their back deck faces the back side of Glacier Point Peak. "And now we have Willem here with us. Which is wonderful, Mom, don't get me wrong! But these are not quite the circumstances anyone had ever imagined, I'm sure, especially after the poor kid just saw his mother's dead body . . . Ooh-Mom, what am I going to do? I have to go talk to Jacob."

Irene placed her hand on Naomi's shoulder, saying nothing. She gave her daughter a genuine, caring smile, and turned to walk away back to the family room where Willem was still lying on the couch.

"How about a game of cards, Grandson?"

CHAPTER 25

THE FUNERAL

The following evening, Rose Carson's mother and step-father arrived at Naomi Willem's house. Shortly after, so did two of Rose's cousins. Irene O'Brien was helping prepare dinner with her daughter in the kitchen, and asked Naomi if she wanted her to stay.

"Mom, more than anything. Please don't leave me now."

Young Willem Carson met his grandparents for the first time, and his mom's cousins that he somewhat remembered. They all retreated to the formal sitting room, awaiting dinner to be ready. There was a lot of silence in the house, with exception to the sound of crying, and pages turning. Rose Carson's parents thumbed through magazines that were on the coffee table, not having read a thing. The cousin's consoled Willem as well they could, but kept asking inappropriate questions which only made the entire ordeal worse for him.

He didn't want to hear the fact that his mom had kept him away from all of them his entire life. He didn't want to hear that his grandparents disapproved of Rose's way of becoming pregnant. They confessed to Willem that they had disowned her for being pregnant out of wedlock. They knew now what a horrible mistake that was. They knew it long ago, but when trying to make amends with their daughter, Rose refused to forgive them.

Willem didn't want to hear any of it. He grew angry, and ran out of the room to be with Irene and Naomi in the kitchen.

Dinner was prepared, and the families sat at the dining room table together, everyone asking questions to Naomi, trying to make sense of the situation. The awkwardness of the dinner conversations took precedence over the fact that Rose was dead. That disgusted Naomi, and she began to regret inviting any of them to stay in her home.

After Rose's parents left that evening to go their hotel, Naomi's mother, Irene, helped make the cousins at home in the spare room, and made up a bed on the sofa for Willem. She herself retired to Naomi and Jacob's bedroom, as Naomi had told her she would sleep in her study that night.

Naomi poured herself a glass of wine, and retreated to the back deck. The chalk outlining was still a fade on the floor, even after her mother had cleaned everything up so well. Tears formed in her eyes at the memory of her friend, and everything else that was going on. She felt overwhelmed and defeated.

Taking in a deep breath, Naomi sat on her porch reflecting on the days past, she felt the cool breeze engulf her energies. The moon was invigorating, so bright, illuminating the silhouette of the mountainside, and highlighting rays through the choppy and sweeping clouds. Chills dressed her skin with goose bumps, and she wrapped herself in her favorite cashmere throw blanket. "The sky is radiant tonight, my love," she said aloud to Jacob as though he was sitting there with her. There was a silence in the air that spoke a million truths. Naomi felt her thoughts becoming clearer. Her body rested calmly in her lounge chair, as her mind reeled along the paths of a dozen rivers, all flowing in their own directions. Releasing the stresses of the week's past, praying for the release of the burdens that weighed them down, she felt so very thankful for the blessings that now kept her breath alive.

Rose's funeral was the following afternoon. It took place at a nearby cemetery, with hills of tombstones surrounding them. It was a small and private event; short, to say the least. Rose Carson's parents, her cousins, Irene O'Brien, young Willem Carson, and Naomi Willem, all stood there together as the minister delivered the eulogy and a prayer for the family in grief. They wore black, and stood still in their silence for a short time after, holding umbrellas as they watched the drizzle of the raindrops fall atop Rose Carson's coffin, and to the green grass below.

Rachelle Wong came to film the funeral. After the ceremony was complete, and people dispersed to their vehicles, she confronted Naomi.

Naomi motioned for her mother to take Willem with her to their car by a simple look and nod of her head, which Irene understood clearly and did in fact do.

Rachelle questioned why her husband, Jacob, was not there. Naomi explained he had been in an accident and was still in the hospital, so he was not able to attend, but that Rose was a dear friend of theirs visiting them at their home. She stopped explaining as she realized her nerves were shot, and she was most likely rambling information to this woman that was none of her business.

"Why are you here, Miss Wong?"

"Well, you see, I have learned that your husband works for the Crione Agency who was undertaking some sort of project up on that mountainside at Glacier Point Peak Pass. And, then I heard about your friend here. Mrs. Willem, my crew and I went up to see what was causing all of those explosions, and the next thing we know, we were being shot at and my friend goes missing." There was a long pause before Rachelle continued. "Mrs. Willem, I believe your husband might know what happened to my friend, and I'd simply like to ask him some questions."

"That's impossible. My husband's been in the hospital for days. And, what do you mean, you found out about my friend? By whom?"

"Well, I'm a reporter, Ma'am, I have my ways," Rachelle responded with a smirk on her face. Rachelle felt like she was enjoying this too much.

"Like I told you, my husband suffered severe injuries in a car accident. Now, if you don't mind, this is a private affair. You really need to leave. I'm sure you can at least understand that."

Rachelle, complying with Naomi's request, turned to walk away to leave. She stopped to look back at Naomi, and inquired aloud, "Mrs. Willem?"

"Yes."

"What did your husband drive? You know, in the accident."

"Our Dodge truck. Why?" Naomi responded.

"Just curious. I heard about that accident on a scanner that night. Thought it might be him. Thank you for your time, Mrs. Willem. And . . . I am truly sorry about your friend. I do hope your husband will be okay."

Naomi nodded in Rachelle's direction, a nod to say, "Thank you and you may leave now."

Rachelle returned to her van, realizing that Jacob Willem was the man at the accident site where Joe was killed. Visions of that day flooded her mind. She was convinced now that Jacob Willem had something to do with Steve's murder. Paranoid, she concluded that Jacob must have been following them somehow, and that he must have been on his way to the hospital where Rachelle had taken Joe. This couldn't simply be a coincidence, she convinced herself, and she was damned if she was going to keep silent about it. She called and told her boss everything that had happened, and the connections she had concocted. He told her to run with it.

Later that night, Naomi turned on the news; Feeling nervous about the reporter who had asked her about Jacob earlier that day at Rose's funeral.

Rachelle Wong was on TV, and in her news casting she reported a suspected attachment between "this woman's killer and the events on Glacier Point Peak Pass," while airing footage of Rose's funeral, with white bold lettering casted across the bottom of the screen, "ROSE CARSON FOUND DEAD AT A CRIONE EMPLOYEE's HOME." Rachelle ended her piece with the unanswered whereabouts of her cameraman man, Steve Maders, requesting anyone who knew anything about his whereabouts, to contact the News Station immediately.

Disgusted, and feeling quite irritated at this news anchor's accusations, Naomi turned the TV off, and stormed out of the house to get some air. "Who the hell is this woman anyway?" She yelled aloud to herself. "Where does she get off making such claims about my husband on air like that?" Taking a deep breath in, she slowly exhaled. Her next thought drifted off . . . "And, where is Steve Maders? What does he have to do with any of this?"

CHAPTER 26

NOTHING MORE

Still in the hospital, a day after Rose's funeral, Jacob's treatments were showing effective results, and he was being removed from quarantine status. Still a suspect and not yet questioned, Jacob was surprised not to have heard from anyone, and worried why the police hadn't been back to talk to him. Had they found Calister and Borgam? Just as that thought ran through his mind, the door to his room opened. He expected the worst, but instead was shocked to see his father, Richard Willem, walk through the door.

Richard visited with Jacob in the hospital for hours. He told him of his involvement with the Crione Agency . . . explaining that's why they moved to Omaha all those years ago; he and Frank Calister had been in the forces together; attended college together, and had been long time friends. Richard told him that it was his influence that had gotten Jacob into Cambridge but that Calister would not have hired him if he didn't believe in Jacob, too.

Jacob sat in silence, listening to everything his father explained. He was in shock. It was all too unbelievable, too unreal.

Richard continued, and pleaded with Jacob to flee the country with him to meet Calister at the new project site in France. Jacob couldn't fathom the idea of leaving now. He told his father about Willem. "You have a grandson, Dad. I have a son, and I haven't even met him yet. How could I leave now?"

Richards's demeanor changed as he asked Jacob for forgiveness for lying to him all those years, and for not telling him about his involvement with the project for Crione. Jacob, feeling angry and betrayed, ignored those emotions and begged his father for protection.

Jacob told him that he must live past all of this; that he had to afford the time with his son, to make a life for him, for Willem, and Naomi. "Dad, there's something else. Someone tried to kill Naomi. They already killed Rose. You remember Rose, don't you? She's the mother of my son. Dad . . . . I'm scared. We're all scared. I think Frank's involvement is deeper than you know. Or, do you know?" Jacob paused, staring coarsely at his father, a man before him that he no longer felt he truly knew. "Dad, you would tell me, right? Was Frank Calister the one who tried to kill my wife?"

Richard sat in silence listening to his son plea for his life, and any understanding to the mess around him. Richard shook his head as if to say no. He couldn't muster any words.

Jacob continued, frustrated by his father's sudden silence, and told him that Clint Borgam tried to kill him in his bed right there in the hospital. "I'm afraid that Calister is after me next."

Richard patted his son's head, caressing his hair with his hand, and assured Jacob that he had Calister under control. Jacob grew angry, his lips quivering with angst. Richard begged him for forgiveness. He told Jacob he did not want to lose him, and assured him he would fix everything that had gone wrong. Jacob told his father to leave and get out of his life for good. "How could you? How could you do this, be a part of all of this chaos? Who are you? You have to leave . . . I can't bare your presence right now."

Richard nodded, and agreed to leave, but first told Jacob that he had a flight to prepare for. "I'm meeting Calister at the project site in a day or two. I'll be staying at a local hotel in Ballard in the meantime. We have to salvage the weapons and tanks in the container room before we can leave. Hopefully Borgam didn't destroy it all in the explosion before Calister took care of him, you know?" Richard stood to leave. He took Jacob's hand, and looked him in the eye. "Son, I'm so very sorry. I'm just so sorry."

"What about Krindle?" Jacob asked as he pulled his hand away.

"I'll tell you about him another time. He seems to have taken himself out of the picture, not answering anyone's calls. It's almost like he's disappeared."

After Richard left, Jacob called home to talk to his mom, Florence. He wanted to know whether she had known the truth. "Jacob, my handsome son . . . all your dad told me is that he was going on a work trip to France, somewhere near Paris, with Frank. A matter of fact, he was here the other night."

"Who? Who was there, Mom?"

"Frank. Yes, I made supper. We ate, and your dad showed him his office. Jacob, what is this all about?" Feeling suddenly frantic with worry, Florence continued, "I didn't even know Dad went to see you! Are you alright, Son? Are you in pain? Are you in danger?"

Jacob told her everything. He told her that his dad was involved in a cover up for the accidents that occurred at his project site, that he actually works for Crione Agency and that was why Jacob was even accepted into Cambridge, and the reason he had his job at Crione. Florence listened silently before interrupting, "I've had my suspicions over the years, son, but . . . I never wanted to admit it was the truth. You know your dad hasn't talked to me about his work, well not in detail, in over fifteen years? He's a scientist, that's all I know . . . honestly, Son. That's the sad truth of it."

"Mom, he's in the middle of a deal to sell nuclear warheads to a group of men in France. He set me up . . . set me up with this job so I could build safety tanks to hold the weapons in, and prepare them for delivery at any given moment. Mom, he's going to get caught. As soon as authorities figure out he's involved, Calister will throw him under the buss. Whatever you do, don't trust Frank Calister. He's already trying to pin everything on me. For god sakes, Mom, Dad tried to have Naomi killed!"

They spoke on the phone for quite some time. Jacob told her about Rose, and her grandson . . . "We'll fly out after things calm down so you can meet Will in person. Right now," Jacob told her, "I just need to protect my family. And, Mom, please be careful."

Jacob and Florence exchanged sentiments of "I love you" and hung up their phones.

Shortly after, Detective Morris and Officer Harris entered Jacob's room. They began their long awaited questioning. Jacob insisted he was only in charge of designing holding tanks for military weapons, and the training of a safety crew for tunnel digging. He explained there had been an accident at the project site, and all of his crew members were buried alive. He said he was not told any details, and did not know what exactly happened, or why. "I only do my job, and follow orders," Jacob lied, and continued to say, "I've never even been to the project site. I know it's in the mountain up at the Pass. Apparently it's hard to access." Jacob continued to explain that all of his work was done from his office, and that the training took place in the development room at Crione Agency.

Jacob explained that, of course, being that he worked for Crione, he knew the engineering was designed for nuclear warheads, but as far as he knew, they were inactive shells. "That's what I was told. This was a testing project for safety procedures. I can tell you how to get there, but I . . ."

The detectives interrupted, telling Jacob they had already been to Crione Agency. They'd been in his office and found documents in Frank Calister's safe box about the project site, which they had also been to. They threatened Jacob with life in prison if he did not comply and tell them the truth, asking him when he planned on meeting with Mr. Calister next.

Jacob insisted that he wasn't the one who set up that meeting with Calister; "I don't know who did!" he lied again, as his Father had just confessed to him about their flight to Paris that would take place in the next couple of days.

"Mr. Willem, who is Clint Borgam?"

"He is my commanding superior."

"Do you know the whereabouts of Calister or Borgam now, or why they are seemingly M.I.A.?"

Jacob was surprised to hear Calister was missing. "All I know about Borgam is that he was supposed to seal off the tunnel at the project site for safety precautions." Jacob responded while he shook his head "no," and insisted he had no idea where they were, and had not heard from them since before the accident at the project site.

Jacob's breath suddenly shortened, and his heart rate was registering too high. Nurses rushed in, pushing the detectives aside. One told them that they would have to leave.

Detective Moore and Officer Harris decided to head to that mountain. When they arrived at Glacier Point Peak Pass, they discovered the sealed off tunnel that was accomplished apparently by the final explosions Clint Borgam had been in charge of. Still searching for Calister & Krindle, and with nothing around themselves except piles of rocky debris and large boulders from the explosions, they decided they really didn't know what they were looking for there. In the distance, Harris noticed a smooth area in the dirt where trees had been cut down, the burned areas that were neatly cleaned up. She pointed out to Moore that there were no tracks to prove what had gone on there. It seemed all evidence had been covered up, and they knew if they wanted any answers, they would have to find a way to get into that tunnel.

Orders for tractors and rescue crews were on their way. It took days of digging before they could inspect the interior of this said project site within this tunnel on a mountainside.

When the tunnel was finally exposed, they discovered burned bodies, weapons, tanks, etc., but not the containment room. They found and identified Clint Borgam's shot body down the hillside, though. One missing link, one missing person was accounted for, but they still didn't have the answers.

The following day they decided to return to question Jacob Willem.

"Your boss' body was found dead."

"Who?"

"Your boss, you know, Clint Borgam. You said he was your boss, right?"

"He is my commanding superior, yes." Jacob in disbelief, turned pale as a ghost. Scared out of his mind, he started to sweat.

"Anything else you feel like telling us now, Mr. Willem?"

Jacob did not respond.

"Tell us when you are meeting with Frank Calister! We can't protect you or your family if you don't tell us the truth. Just tell us why you plan on going to France with Calister!" Detective Moore pressed.

"Protect me?" Jacob's anger with the entire situation surfaced. "Protect my family?" He let out a laugh, "Ha!" Jacob shook his head in disbelief of their involvement, and said, "You tell me that Clint Borgam is dead, that Frank Calister is planning a trip somewhere out of the country, and then threaten my life with prison, all in the same conversation! How stupid do you think I am?" Feeling as though he was acting even more suspicious, he calmed himself, took in a deep breath, and continued, "Listen guys, if you're not here to arrest me, then please, just let me get my rest. I'm too tired for all of this. I just want to go home to my family. If you really want to help, then protect my family! Please."

Detective Moore, in an attempt to make one last effort to pry information from Jacob's tired mind, offered to make a deal with him if he would tell them everything, "every last detail, from beginning to us standing here in front of you."

Jacob swore on his life that he knew nothing else.

"I wouldn't be throwing around debts on your own life so easily, Mr. Willem. It seems there are enough dead bodies around you already."

"Are you threatening me?" Jacob asked.

"No, just a little advice, Mr. Willem, just a little advice."

"Listen, if you're not arresting me, and if there's nothing more you have to tell me now, please, just leave." Exhausted, Jacob turned his head against his pillow to rest. He closed his eyes, and fell asleep before Detective Moore and Officer Harris could even leave his room.

Realizing now that they would be forced to release him as a suspect if they didn't arrest him, Moore and Harris told Jacob's nursing staff to notify them as soon as he was stable enough to leave the hospital. Officer Harris handed the nurse their business card as they left the hospital once more.

CHAPTER 27

HERO IRENE

It had been days since Naomi had been to see Jacob in the hospital. She was consumed with her mixed emotions: feelings of confusion about her marriage, all the lies, the deceit, surrounding dangers, and being scared for their lives. She did not want to leave Willem's side either, and was doing all she could to avoid the detectives, as well as trying to focus on her work; it was all weighing heavy on her shoulders. She needed to process. She needed time, but time was not on her side, so she decided it to turn to Irene for help.

"Mom, I need you now more than I ever have before."

"Anything for you, my darling. What is it?" Irene inquired.

"Well, I just have so many things racing through my mind. My gallery show is coming up soon, you know, and there are so many details to still settle . . . and with Jacob so ill, and not here to help me with Willem. He doesn't even know about him yet, Mom. Did I tell you that?" Naomi wondered why she still felt the need to lie about that aspect to her Mom. Shaking her head side to side to wave away those thoughts for now, she continued, "And, he's not here to help get us through all of this mess . . ." Naomi's nerves were shot; darkened circles had claimed their position under her eyes and her hands, she could not stop the shaking; they confessed her every emotion. "Mom, I cannot thank you enough for all you have done these last few days."

Irene took Naomi's hand and placed it in her own. As she patted the top of her daughter's hand, she responded, "Oh, Naomi, my sweet daughter. Your plate is definitely full. I love being able to be here . . . and, Willem, young Will. He is a fine young man. You know, he's pretty funny, that boy. You go do . . . whatever it is you need to do. I have nowhere to go. Take your time. We will be fine. Don't you worry one bit!"

"I need to talk with Jacob, Mom. I need to check in on him. Do you think I should tell him about Willem? You know . . . umm, I mean, I know you don't care for him, but he's my . . . . he's my . . . ."

Irene interrupted Naomi, "I know that I have not been very supportive of your marriage to Jacob, but in all honesty, I think I have been jealous of you, Naomi. Your marriage to that man has certainly lasted longer than any relationship I have ever given a chance after your father left us." Tears forming in Irene's eyes, her voice softening even more, she continued, "I am just so very sorry for that. I thought I had convinced myself that my hatred towards men would protect you from them. I am learning now that it has simply blinded me from truly knowing what love is. I never want you to know what being truly alone feels like. You and Jacob were meant for one another, my darling. Go to him. He needs you, too."

Uncontrollable silent tears fell from their faces. All they could do was to stare at one another, holding hands, reading each other's souls. They sat that way for several minutes until Irene smiled at Naomi. She placed her hands on Naomi's face; her palms caressed over her ears, and wiped Naomi's tears aside with her thumbs. Irene sat up straight, shook her head side to side as if to shake away a bee flying in front of her face, wiped her own tears away, and told Naomi, "You go on now. We'll be fine.'

Naomi gave her mother a long hug, gathered her essentials, and left to see Jacob at St. Jude's Hospital.

When Naomi arrived at the hospital to be with Jacob, she confronted him about all of her concerns about his work, and her fears now that someone tried to kill her. She cried with him about Rose, and told him about the funeral, and how the reporter had come and questioned her. "She aired on the news for god's sake, Jacob! She thinks you have something to do with her cameraman being missing!" Naomi continued to explain that the police had been to the house again, questioning her about Crione and Jacob's involvement.

A deep sigh of relief released from Jacob, as he realized that very moment that the love of his life was sitting terrified in front of his ill body, and that he was finally going to tell her the truth: The truth about everything.

And so he did. Jacob slowly began from the beginning, from

Cambridge, and meeting Rose at that bar. He assured her that he had known nothing of Willem's existence. Breaking down in tears, Naomi could see his genuine nature showing itself once again. She knew that moment he was telling her the truth.

Jacob explained when they first moved to Darrington, when he first started working for Crione Agency, and what his role truly was there. He told her about the explosions, and described why he'd been as shocked as she was when they heard them for the first time. He explained that phone call before he left that night, and that he had rushed to the project site on Glacier Point Peak Pass, all of the dead bodies, weapons, the nuclear warheads, overseas private buyers, the government's involvement in funding their project, how the police found Borgam's body, and that they believed Frank Calister was the one who killed him. He told her that Calister was missing or out of the country already. "Naomi, there was chaos everywhere up there. It was an accident though. My crew . . . they messed up somehow. They're all dead. Naomi, I swear to you. Something went horribly wrong."

Jacob continued with his explanation. Naomi sat in silence, engulfed in his story, waiting for it all to come together, for all of it to make sense. Why Rose? Why was she dead? Naomi realized that was all coincidental, and quickly blamed herself for Rose's death. "If I hadn't called her . . . if she wasn't at our house, she wouldn't have died, Jacob! That man was after me, not her . . ."

"Naomi . . . but then we would have never known about Willem. This isn't your fault. The fault is all mine. My hands are covered in blood with all of this. For god sake, Naomi, I helped carry dead bodies to the containment room. We burned it all . . . all of them. It's just all out of control. I don't know what else to do. Please, Naomi . . . I can't lose you now. Please . . . please, forgive me."

"Ooh-no . . . is he after you next? Who was it? Who was that man in our house, Jacob?"

"Frank Calister."

"How do you know for sure?"

"Naomi, my dad came to see me."

"Richard? What? When?"

"Here, in the hospital."

Naomi's confused expression urged him to continue. She had no words. She did not know what Jacob was trying to tell her now.

"My joy . . . He wants me to meet him at the airport in a couple of days. Police are having the site at the Pass dug out for investigations." He paused before speaking more, perhaps waiting for her to piece the puzzle together so he didn't have to say it aloud. "Then when the coast is clear, I guess, that is when they'll sneak in to retrieve whatever remaining warheads exist up there. He wants . . . he wants me to go to France with him and Calister."

"What . . . well, what did you tell him?"

"I refused. I told him to get out of my life." Jacob turned his head towards the window. He could no longer look his wife in the eyes. "Naomi, my dad is the one who tried to have you killed. Calister's the one who pulled the trigger."

Naomi stood, and walked slowly towards that window her husband now stared out of. She felt a surge of energy pass through her body. Not an energy rush as though she had drank too much coffee, but a deep seething sensation within her. It nearly cooled her veins. She could feel her fears dissipate, and she realized that from this moment on, life would never be the same as they'd known it to be. She knew this moment that she was a changed woman. Her mind felt clear. Her thoughts, crisp. She felt focused, and strong.

"We'll cover it up," she told Jacob. "We're not involved directly. That is what you will continue to say."

Jacob stared at this woman speaking to him from in front of the window; her silhouette seemingly taller, statuette, and radiant. This was the girl he had once seen through that art studio's window when they were so young. This was his wife. He was more drawn to her now than he remembered ever feeling.

Naomi still talking, Jacob tried to focus his attention to her words. "With Calister missing, Clint Borgam dead, and your crew dead . . . your dad leading this whole mess, no one can ever know you were involved, at least not hands on. You can say that Crione set you up. Calister and Tommy Krindle set this entire thing up to make you their target. They want you to take the fall for their screw ups anyhow! You being held in the dark would not be unbelievable, you know?" With a shrug of her shoulders, Naomi told Jacob, "You've done nothing illegal if they only know about your engineering sealant tank holders for the military warhead shells . . . or weapons, whatever you called them."

Pacing now, a few silent moments had passed between them, Jacob admiring his wife in motion, Naomi came to a quick halt, staring at her husband, she asked, "But, where exactly is Calister now?"

"I honestly don't know. Dad said something about a new project site in Paris. Naomi, you have to find him before he finds us . . . before he finds Will. He'll do anything to clear his name and bury evidence . . . bury us. I'm afraid . . . afraid he'll go after my dad next." Jacob broke down in tears, shoulders shaking, sobbing uncontrollably all the sudden. His strength was weak from being so sick for so long. "I told him I didn't want anything to do with him, Naomi. I told him to get out of our lives for good," he stated in disbelief.

Naomi, trying her best to be understanding and patient, replied, "Honey . . . your dad has made some major mistakes, too. He's risked our lives. He tried to take mine. Rose is dead because of him. I know you have made your mistakes, too. It seems both of your hands are bloody, I know, but if you want Richard back in our lives, that is up to you . . . but, you promise me that man will never step foot in our home again, and that I will never have to see him again, be in the same room with him . . . ever again. Promise me."

"Naomi, I don't know that I am ready to forgive him, but that doesn't mean that I want him dead!"

"Did Richard put the mark on Borgam?"

"I really don't think he did, Naomi. I don't think my Dad meant for any of this to happen. It's just spiraled out of control, and reacted to . . . well, to cover up his own ass. To cover mine."

CHAPTER 28

GALLERY EVENT, TWO
WEEKS LATER

Frank Calister walked steadily into the gallery where Naomi was holding her art exhibition. He told her he had come to offer his condolences about her friend Rose. "I have been overseas, and when I found out about your friend, and all the troubles that have occurred in recent weeks, I felt I needed to make a personal visit with you. When I saw that you were having an art show here, I just had to stop in. You're a talented woman, Naomi. How is Jacob doing these days? Is he recovering? Will he be home with you soon?"

Shaken, Naomi responded as calmly as she could, "Thank you, Frank . . . Jacob's still in the hospital. I . . . I appreciate you coming by. We . . . we've all been concerned about you. Is there . . . anything else you need? I really need to get back to . . ." she gestured to the crowd of people surrounding them admiring her paintings.

"Well, yes, actually there is. This one here. I'd like this one. Cash." Calister nodded his head towards the painting displayed before them, secured to a wall of its own. The painting Naomi had painted that regretted night that she'd attempted to take her own life. The night Rose was shot to death on the back deck of her and Jacob's home. The night the man, in front of her now, had tried to kill her.

Naomi made the arrangements for her painting to be delivered to Frank Calister's home. She knew it was strange that he was there, but she didn't miss a beat. She told him they were worried not having heard from him and told him she was thankful for his appreciation in her art, and that he had just purchased her favorite piece. "I hope you enjoy it," she told

Calister, continuing to tell him that she and Jacob hoped he was well, and explained that Jacob would probably be in the hospital a little while longer. "He's in bad condition after the car accident, Frank, and well, for having been so ill these last months because of the radiation he was exposed to . . . we're not sure he'll make it through this one, honestly."

There was a long awkward pause as Calister studied Naomi's face, watching carefully her eyes and lips as she spoke candidly with him. He calculated the situation to contemplate what he should do with her. Not caring that Richard Willem had already told him that Naomi was no longer a risk, he had to know for himself.

Naomi interrupted the silence with a smile, "Well, thank you. I apologize for rambling a bit . . . I guess I haven't had anyone to really talk to these days. Thank you, again, so much, for coming by, and for taking interest in my work."

Calister found himself distracted by just how attractive Naomi was, leaning to offer her a hug. She could barely stand it, but allowed the embrace. The hug was slightly longer than a normal one among acquaintances should be, and Naomi realized he needed to leave. She pulled away from his arms, and told him, "Everything will be alright, I'm sure. You be careful out there, Frank. The police have been asking a lot of questions. The last I heard, they were still looking for you." Frank Calister responded with a slight smirk on his face, saying no more, he took a step towards the front door of the gallery showroom.

Wanting to test his response, Naomi added, softly spoken, "Ooh, and Frank . . . thanks for taking care of Borgam."

Taken aback by Naomi's remark, he stood silent for a moment. Calister figuring his old pal, Richard, must have spoken with Jacob and Naomi, he felt at ease that he could now believe that the Willems' were no longer a threat to him. While holding up his receipt with a flirtatious smile, he responded, "I guess this makes us even."

Naomi had no idea what he meant by that, so simply said, "Goodbye, Frank."

Calister took a step back towards her, grasped her shoulders in his large strong hands. Leaning his body in towards hers, he kissed Naomi's cheek, whispering, "You can call me for anything . . . anytime."

She felt like she was going to vomit that very moment. Smiling instead, she thanked him once more and watched him walk away, and out of her sight.

Shaken by the whole ordeal, she realized she wasn't breathing. Naomi let out a big sigh of relief, a release from deep within her lungs, and feeling as though she knew there was a purpose that she was still alive. She walked towards the back of her gallery showroom to gather her composure before returning to her guests.

Willem Carson was also there with Naomi at the gallery event. Hidden behind a large wall that held another painted canvass Naomi had displayed, he had watched her with the tall man.

When Frank Calister left, having regained her composure, Naomi noticed young Willem behind her painting. She walked over to him. He was frozen still, had wet his pants, and was shaking uncontrollably. Willem stared at her with fright in his eyes. "Who is that man?" he asked.

"That man's name is Frank Calister, Will. He is your dad's boss . . . but, he's a bad man." Naomi paused, placing her arm around her new son. "Will, I don't have to tell you that though, do I?"

Willem told Naomi that Calister was the man that shot her, and killed his mother. He told Naomi that he had told the police about him, and given them his license plate number. "The police didn't tell you?" Willem inquired.

Naomi, in shock that she hadn't considered the impact on Willem with Calister being there, quickly grew angry at herself. How had she been so blind to allow that man there while Willem was in the back? She replied simply that she knew everything already that Willem had just told her, but tried to assure him that police officers were handling it, and that they had told her to be calm if she ever saw him again. "I'll call them later and tell them he was here, okay? You don't have to be scared anymore, Will. I wish I could bring your mom back, I do, so badly. She was my best friend. But, I'm going to take care of all of this. If it's the last breath I take, that man will be punished for what he's done."

She took Willem in her arms, and explained she had to sell Calister her painting so she could give the police his address. She knew she was lying to him, but she knew it was only to protect him. She told him that Calister didn't know that they all knew who he was. "Come on, Sweetie, let's get you cleaned up."

Naomi told her assistants that she needed to take Willem home, giving instructions on how to run the rest of her event. "I'll check in with you after a bit," she told them.

At home, Naomi thought to call the police about Frank Calister showing up at her gallery event, but quickly placed the phone back on its receiver. She picked the phone back up, and called the hospital instead, requesting a visit with Jacob. Considering the hour, she wanted to make sure security would let her in after visiting hours.

Shortly after, Naomi was at the hospital with Jacob. "Frank Calister came to my gallery show. He purchased a painting to be delivered to his house here in Vancouver. Willem saw him. Jacob, the police can't know that we know where he is. Calister thinks we're on his side. He has no idea that we know that he tried to kill me or that he killed Rose. He definitely did not see Will there, and I don't suspect that he even knew Will saw him leave our house that night. You can't tell the detectives about any of this. Frank Calister will blame everything on you if they find him."

Jacob only nodded his head, exhausted from his treatments. He quickly fell out, and Naomi kissed his forehead and whispered, "I'm going to be leaving for a few days."

Jacob managed to open his eyes enough to focus as well as he could on his wife, she seemed to glow sitting there beside him, an angel, he thought. "What are you going to do?"

Naomi responded vaguely, "I'll call you when I get back, okay?"

"My joy, please be careful. Don't do anything irrational."

"Jacob, nothing at this point in our lives is rational. I'll call you soon."

"What about Willem?"

"I'll have my mom stay with him while I am gone."

"Irene is still here?"

"Yes. Actually, I'm thinking of asking her to take Willem home with her for a few days. You wouldn't believe what a huge help she has been."

"Ya, I'm sure." Jacob retorted sarcastically.

"She apologized to me, Jacob. She finally said she was sorry for not supporting us. She is worried about you, and for us. Give her a chance. I think she is ready to give you another one."

"I love you, Naomi."

"I . . . I love you, too. More than you'll ever know."

"Naomi . . . Are we okay?"

With a wide smile, her eyes softened, as she whispered, "We are, Baby. We will be. I'll call you soon."

CHAPTER 29

DISCOVERY

Another search warrant was granted, allowing Detective Moore and Officer Harris to return to Crione Agency. Searching the offices of Jacob Willem, Frank Calister, the research rooms, and labs, they gathered everything they could find, anything that would create more pieces to their puzzle.

They still needed to figure out a way to link their suspicions about the explosions on Glacier Point Peak Pass with the murder of Clint Borgam, Tommy Krindle's involvement and sudden disappearance, Rose Carson being shot to death next to the attempted killing of Naomi Willem in their own house; the news anchor, Rachelle Wong's crew member, Steve Maders who was missing, Jacob Willem's illness and car accident, where Frank Calister was hiding, what was in France, what were these so called "holding tanks" exactly holding, and how exactly this Crione Agency was responsible for all of it. They were convinced that Jacob Willem was the key to their answers. "How do we link all of this together?" Moore said aloud frustratingly to Officer Harris.

After digging into the pasts of Jacob and Naomi Willem, they knew where they went to school, when they moved to Washington, and that they were from Omaha. They discovered their parents' names, and more travel logs for one Frank Calister and Willem. After discovering that Frank Calister had recently traveled to Omaha, the posing question then became, "Why? Why did Frank Calister go to Omaha?"

"Jacob's father is Richard Willem," Harris told Moore.

"That's right, Darlin'. So, what's your point?"

"Moore, look at the facts. Jacob Willem works for Crione, claims he never set foot on the Pass, knew nothing about anything, only followed his so called orders, and built some sort of holding tank. He's ill, and tight lipped. His wife was almost killed. Their friend was shot to death. He denies any direct involvement. So, maybe he's playing dumb, we don't really know that. But, what if . . . . what if he really is the dumb one here?"

Moore stared blankly at Harris, "Go on, now, where ya' going with this?"

"Calister flew to Omaha days after the explosions, and people go missing. His number one engineer, and his wife, are both hospitalized at the same time, for different reasons, while this Clint Borgam and Tommy Krindle guy both go missing. We find Borgam's body; where's Krindle's? We know Frank Calister is alive even though he is still nowhere to be found. Then, we find these," she held up the travel logs to show Moore.

Officer Harris continued, "Frank Calister went to Omaha. Jacob Willem's parents still live in Omaha. Jacob's father is Richard Willem. I am telling you, Moore, Frank Calister and Richard Willem are our men."

"Shit, Darlin'. You're onto something' good here. How did we miss it? We've gotta find this Calister character."

"How about a trip to Omaha to see Richard Willem?" Harris suggested.

"Right. He's probably long gone. Let's call his house and talk to his wife." Moore fumbled through paperwork. "Florence, is it?" Moore mumbled questionably.

"Alright then," Harris answered, "and what about Calister? Do you think Richard Willem and Frank Calister are hiding out together somewhere?"

"No way to know until we ask some more questions," Moore responded.

"If Calister booked those flights for him and Richard Willem, and not Jacob Willem, then how do we determine why Calister had even flown to Omaha to visit Richard in the first place? There's nothing here that reflects what or if Richard Willem is involved, except that Calister met with him. We need answers. Why don't you pay a visit to Jacob in the hospital to question him about his father while I get a hold of the mother, Florence?" Harris stated to Moore.

"I'm on it, Darlin'," Detective Moore tossed a wink at Officer Harris, holstered his gun, straightened his badge, and with keys in hand, was out the door.

At the hospital, the nurse, beginning to feel as though their patient was being somewhat harassed, answered the Detectives questions about Jacob's visitors, and his status. She informed Detective Moore that Jacob

Willem's father had been there to visit him, as well as his wife recently, but that even though Jacob was stable, he was still very weak. She told Moore to make his visit short.

Jacob Willem, still denying he knew anything, especially anything about his own father's involvement, acted shocked and depressed from the news. He admitted that his dad had, in fact, just been there to visit him.

"Why is your father here in Washington, Mr. Willem?" Moore continued his questioning.

"To see me. I'm in the hospital, in case you haven't noticed . . ." Jacob answered sarcastically. Feeling annoyed by the entire process, he asked Detective Moore if they'd found Tommy Krindle yet.

"We have not. We've issued an arrest warrant though. He's definitely still listed as a suspect. So is your friend, Frank Calister."

"He is not my friend." Jacob let that slip.

The detective stood there in Jacob's room, now in silence, feeling as though perhaps the man in front of him was telling him the truth, at least for the most part. He wondered if Jacob was scared and maybe covering up information because he feared for his own life in this scenario. He wondered if Richard Willem had hidden his role in all of this from Jacob.

"What is your relationship with your father like, Jacob?"

"What do you mean?"

"Do you fight often? Do you know each other well? Are you close?"

"We're close . . . like any other family, I suppose. Visits on the holidays, phone calls to check in and say hello now and then. We definitely visit each other if another one is sick or IN THE HOSPITAL!" Jacob answered frustratingly.

"Does your father work for Crione Agency?" Moore pressed on.

"All I know about my father is that he is a scientist. He worked for a college all my life, for all I know." Jacob's answer drifted off as he realized that moment, even more than before, that he really did not know his father. "I really don't know him that well at all, now that you bring it up . . . . at least not about his work." Jacob paused. "Why are you asking me about my dad anyway?"

Considering exactly what to tell him, Moore decided to plant a seed to test Jacob's response. "Frank Calister visited your father in Omaha recently. We want to know why."

Jacob, remembering his conversation with his mother, carefully decided to answer, "Yeah, he and my father have been friends for years. They went to college together. He flies out for dinners often. I'd guess that's why he went out there . . . . Fly wherever you want, when you want . . . . being rich must be a nice thing, aye?"

"You just said you don't know your father very well. How would know that?"

"I only know that Calister went for dinner because that's what my dad told me when he came to visit me. I guess Calister told him I was here or something."

"Jacob. You've gotta be straight with me, man. Where are your father and Calister now?"

"I honestly do not know," Jacob answered. "If I did, I would tell you. If you knew, I hope you would tell me. It seems you and I have the same kind of questions."

Meanwhile, Naomi returned to her gallery. It was the next afternoon already. Time had taken its own course on the speedway. Her event was over, doors were locked tight, and all of the lights were off. Not a soul was around. The streets were silent, and no cars were parked on the street outside except for hers. She felt like the stars were aligned just right, and only for her. She pulled the delivery ticket from the receipt file for the painting Calister purchased. On it was his address in Vancouver, Washington. She put it in her pocket book, gathered some supplies, and hurried away in her car.

Nearly four hours later, Naomi pulled her car in front of Frank Calister's home. Idling in front of his huge mansion like home, she decided then that she would go through with her plan.

She pulled around to the side of his house, drove about a block, and parked across the street. Lowering her visor, she freshened her makeup in the vanity mirror, closed it, and loosened the top button of her blouse. She patted her hair, turned off her engine, and took in a deep breath. Grabbing her bag, she exited her car and walked slowly towards the front door.

Frank Calister, though surprised at who was standing at his front door step, felt delighted to see her, and welcomed her in. Naomi stepped cautiously into his home. She followed him through the corridors and hallways, to his overly extravagant den. The light was dim, and air felt warm. The scent of burning wood arrogated the room, as though just another living element this man in front of her had taken advantage of. Sure it was only firewood, but to Naomi, he didn't deserve even that, much less the oxygen that he breathed.

The painting that he had purchased from her hung above his fireplace. She hadn't realized how large it was. It covered half his wall.

Frank Calister turned to Naomi, taking her hand in his, and spoke to her. "I was expecting you. I knew we both felt it . . . that connection . . . You are a beautiful woman, Naomi."

Calister led her closer to the fireplace, where they stood embraced.

"Frank, do you know where Tommy Krindle is?" Naomi whispered in his ear.

Caressing her face with his hand, Frank Calister confided in her, explaining that he was the founder of Crione Agency. Continuing his explanations, he lied and told her that Tommy Krindle had most likely escaped to France out of fear for failing at his job. Calister told Naomi that he, too, had been wondering Tommy's whereabouts. "But, none of that matters now," he told her, "I'll find him, and I will take care of him. You need not worry anymore." He leaned in to kiss Naomi's neck. "I haven't stopped thinking of you since I left your gallery expose. You are a stunning woman, Naomi, so sensual, so damn sexy. I must have you." In actuality, he thought to himself, it was when he had visited her home to kill her—that was then when he realized how beautiful she was and that he wanted her for himself.

Naomi took his face in her hands, allowing her hands to caress down his neck. She kissed him back. Frank ran the tip of his tongue from her ear, down her neck, and over her healing scar from where he had shot her. Kissing her skin softly, he felt his manhood come erect. He pulled her blouse down off of her shoulders, his hands passing over her breasts as he began to kiss her nipples slowly, and then hugged her body close against his. They embraced, and kissed long and hard, Frank moaning intensely with pleasure.

Massaging the palm of her hands across his manliness, Naomi whispered to Frank, "I followed you home here, I'm sorry . . . I just felt like you could keep me safe. Ooh, Frank," she kissed him more. "I'm afraid of Jacob, what he'll do. I know what a powerful man you are, Frank . . . . I know you can protect me, right?" Naomi hugged him tighter, allowing her naked breasts to press against his chest, and he whispered in response to her, "Ooh, baby, I'll take care of you, alright."

Kissing longer more, Naomi's hands groping against Frank's hard erection, up and down until she could smell his juices dripping beneath his clothes, she unbuckled his belt. She unzipped his fly, and allowed his pants drop to the floor. Her hands between his boxers and skin, she ran her hands across his firm ass, as she pulled his boxers to the floor. Frank, anxiously unbuttoning his shirt, leaned in to kiss her once more. She led Frank's hands onto her waist and allowed him to pull her nearer still. It was in that moment; Naomi quickly pulled a knife from her jeans pocket, holding it straight at his stomach while he pulled her tight against his body.

The knife pierced Frank Calister's skin, blood gushed over Naomi's tight fist, as an expression of shock shattered the moment across Frank's face. Pulling the tie from his neck, Frank quickly grabbed Naomi towards him, wrapping his tie around her neck, and across her throat. Standing nearly naked, completely vulnerable, and now injured, he began to strangle her. Angered, he screamed, "I should've finished you off when I had the chance, you whore!"

Naomi struggled fiercely, awakening strength inside of her. With knife still in hand, she managed to jab it upward, stabbing him squarely in the side of his neck. Frank dropped loose the tie and fell to his knees. Grabbing for her, he reached his hand outwards as she stepped back to avoid his touch and watched him fall to the ground.

Naomi whispered, "No, now . . . now, we are even."

She stood above him, watching him slowly die. Feeling completely alert, a surge of power had taken hold of her. She felt accomplished, and surprisingly calm. She walked to Frank's bathroom and showered. After changing into clean clothes she had brought with her (she was impressed just how much she had come prepared,) she cleaned any evidence that may lead to her being there, threw her filthy-Calister-covered-clothes into the fireplace, sprayed them and her painting with lighter fluid that already sat on his mantle, and lit a match.

She watched the fire ignite; one huge roar of an ignition. She watched as her clothes burned away, and the fire on her painting spread to the walls surrounding it. The combustion skipped to the curtains and shelving of books and collectibles. The room quickly in a blaze, she calmly walked out of Frank Calister's house, through the front door where she had entered only minutes before.

Once outside, Naomi scanned the area to see that there were no people in sight. She was not surprised that the streets were calm, so quiet. Feeling a sense of empowerment that she had never known before, she walked in a confident stride down a block to her car, and drove away, never looking back.

Chapter 30

No Hold

Detective Moore, realizing there's nothing solid to hold him to, released Jacob from the suspect list, but warned him to stay in the city.

Jacob, stabilized and surprisingly recovered from what was thought to be detrimental, was able to go home, and so it was. Discharge papers were provided after one last review from the doctors, and Naomi was on her way.

She borrowed her mom's Yukon, and she and Will left to pick Jacob up from the hospital. They all hugged, and cried, as it was finally the first time young Willem was able to meet his Father, Jacob. They headed home. Stevie Ray Vaughan was on the radio, "Walking a Tight Rope."

Will in the backseat with earphones on, Jacob whispered to Naomi, "I don't know what you've done, or where you've gone, but I know what I have done. We have to figure out a way to make all of this wrong, right somehow. We have to stop Calister and Krindle . . . and my . . . my father. I don't know if I can live with this blood on my hands."

Naomi reached for Jacob's thigh, the only part of his body not casted it seemed. She caressed his leg in reassurance. They smiled at each other. "It will all work out, Honey. One day at a time. But look now," she motioned at Will in the background, "We're a family. Finally! A family."

"It's a good day, my Joy, isn't it?" said Jacob aloud. "It's a good day."

When they pulled into their driveway, a police car was parked and Detective Moore was leaning against his trunk. He asked how Jacob was feeling, and told them he hated to be there, but that he'd gotten a concerning call a few days ago from Tami Krindle. "Jacob, she said you may know where her husband is. Who is Tommy Krindle, Mr. Willem? We know he was not just an engineer like you were."

"Perhaps all I know of Tommy . . . is that he loved to drink and he loved his young women. I've never known anything different." Jacob responded.

Jacob's expression was simple exhaustion. Naomi interrupted, looked at her husband, and told both the detective and Jacob that Tami and Tommy Krindle were not friends of theirs. "I had spoken to Tami the day after Jacob's accident. Tami told me then that Tommy hadn't been home the night before. I told you that, Detective! And, everyone knows he was cheating on her. You know, he told me ages ago that he was planning on going to Spain to take an engineering job there. Not sure the name of the company though. He never really said, now that I think about it." Naomi paused before continuing, "I really think Tami is simply in denial. She always knew what was going on in those mountains, she had to! But she refused to tell me anything about it. She acted like she was my friend, but really she was just trying to keep tabs on her husband."

Detective Moore inquired then, "Why do you think Tommy Krindle knew about . . . about all of this?"

"Because," Naomi continued matter of factually, "Detective Moore, Tami told me that Tommy Krindle, her husband, is the founder and private partner of Crione Agency. She's been covering up for him this whole time! I promised I wouldn't say anything, and honestly, I didn't think to mention that part of it when you and I spoke last. Plus, I figured of all people, you would have already known THAT. I was just worried about the safety of my family!"

"Jacob, is any of this true?" inquired Moore.

"Detective, I didn't even know this . . . if Naomi says that's what Tami Krindle told her, then that is what Tami Krindle told her. Like I told you already, you are barking up the wrong tree. Now, if you'll excuse us, I really need to get inside. Will here needs his rest, and so do I, for that matter. We've really been through enough, and more than patient with all of your questioning. Now, please, stop harassing us. Crione is over. Well, at least, I am done there. That's definite."

The detective glanced at the ground a moment, then back up at the Willems, "Well, alright then. If you hear anything else, please call me," as he reached out to hand their boy, Willem Carson, his business card. Naomi intercepted, and grabbed the card from Will, handing it back to Detective Moore, she said, "We already have it. Now please leave."

She took Jacob by his shoulder and grabbed Will's hand in her other, and they began to walk towards their house. As they reached their front steps, Naomi glanced over her shoulder and saw that Detective Moore was following them up their walkway.

Jacob turned slightly, enough to see what Naomi motioned her head toward, and asked aloud to Moore, "What else?"

"Well, see, I almost forgot." Shaking his head, he let out a slight laughter, "You never told me what your father does for a living. Why-now, doesn't he live in Omaha? That's where you're both from, aren't ya's?"

"Listen, I have already answered your questions. He's an industrial scientist, has been for years. You know he lives in Omaha. He's getting ready to leave for a trip for work. He came to see me first because I was in the hospital. That's all I know. Really!"

"And where is he now?"

"I don't know!" Jacob grew increasingly impatient.

"Ya, well, we also know that wherever your father is going, is where Calister's gone to. We have suspicion to believe that your father and Calister are the ones who are responsible for . . ."

Jacob interrupted, "That's ridiculous."

"Ooh, really? Why? Why is it ridiculous to think that your father and Frank Calister are in cohorts together, and that they are the ones solely responsible for these murders? All of the killings, Jacob! All of this bloodshed and the covering up, and explosions! What are you hiding? What did you design those holding tanks for? Is it really worth it? Damn it, where is your father, Jacob?" Moore demanded.

"I already told you. I really do not know. My father doesn't talk much about his work, not to me, not my family, my mom, no one really. He's a private man."

"Hmm. I see. Like father like son." Moore retorted.

"Sure, whatever you say. Are we done here?" Jacob asked.

"Well, I suppose it appears so, doesn't it, Mr. Willem?"

After watching the detective leave, they finally headed inside of the house. After getting Will situated and calmed down, Naomi began to make them all something to eat in the kitchen. Making his way to his den, Jacob called his dad.

"Detective Moore and Officer Harris will be looking for you, Dad. They know too much. Please . . . . just be careful."

"I'm sorry, Son . . ."

"I know, Dad, I know."

Chapter 31

Burned Out

Back at the station, Moore threw his coat on the floor by his desk in frustration, mumbling something aloud to the extent of this ending his career.

Officer Harris watched him calmly, waiting for his temper tantrum to end, she finally interjected to inform him, "Hey, don't be so hard of yourself. While you were out playing catch the mouse with the Willems, I got a tip from Vancouver P.D. Calister apparently owns a home there."

"So? Is he there?" Moore snapped out of frustration.

"Well, someone is. The house has been burned to a crisp, and there's a body."

"Calister?"

"There's only one way to find out. Already had them send out for his dental records, too. Just waiting for a match," Harris answered.

"Come on. We're going on a road trip."

Richard Willem had grown paranoid after the call he had received from his son, Jacob. He, too, was on a road trip.

When Richard arrived at Frank Calister's home in Vancouver, he could not believe his eyes. The place was burned to the studs. Black smoke still smoldering above, fire fighters still on the scene, and the local police had the entire place taped off. He knew those detectives had to be close if not already there. Panicked, Richard assumed that Tommy Krindle must have had Calister killed off, and is convinced that he would be next.

Richard speeds away to a remote location, where he felt safe enough to stop and call Jacob. "I think Krindle killed Calister, Son, and I'm afraid he is after me next. I have to get out of the country, and fast."

"Dad, I'm not their suspect anymore. You are. Krindle is. They're going to charge you with murder, with conspiracy, withholding evidence, you name it! Dad, you're going away for life if they catch you."

"I know, Son. That is why I must leave the country. I'll be free and clear once I get to Paris."

"Who exactly is Krindle, Dad? What does he do? He sure as hell is no engineer." Jacob wanted to hear it from his dad's mouth. "Dad, just tell me the truth. For once in your life, tell me the truth!"

"You're right, Son. He's not just an engineer. Tommy Krindle is the founder of Crione. He owns us!" There was a long pause, and when Jacob did not respond, Richard continued, "I'm leaving for France. This has all gotten beyond my control. I have to go stabilize our new territory. We cannot afford to lose this client. Krindle will have my head if I can't clean up this mess. Please, Son, don't tell your Mom. She knows nothing, I swear to you, and I don't want her to worry."

"I know, Dad, I already called her."

CHAPTER 32

FREEDOM HAS A COST

"Damn it, this feels like connect the dots, except with dead people!" Detective Moore confessed to Officer Harris.

Nodding her head in agreement, she stated, "We're not going to find anything else here besides Calister's dead body, Moore. We have to find Richard Willem. And Krindle."

Out of character, feeling at a total loss, Moore asked, "Darlin', do you think Jacob Willems had anything to do with this fire, and Calister's now very burned, and dead, body? Is he covering his tracks, ya' think?"

Harris was surprised Moore actually asked her opinion, but responded, "Honestly, how could he be? You had to be standing at his doorsteps talking to him when these embers were just being soaked out, right? So before that, he was still in the hospital, where you said his wife and kid were there waiting for him to be discharged. If you really want to know my opinion, Moore, it's his father we need to go after. I'd put money on it that that man had something to do with this fire."

Their conversation was interrupted by Detective Moore's cellular phone. He answered after the fourth ring. Harris watched as Moore stood there just listening to whoever it was on the other line. When he hung up, he stared towards Harris with a wide smirk on his face.

"Well? What was that? What?" Harris inquired with anticipation.

"I don't know who that was, but some woman just answered all of our questions without me saying a word."

"Come on now, man, what is it?"

"Tommy Krindle killed Calister and set this fire. Richard Willem is on his way to France, scared for his life. His plane leaves tomorrow morning out of Seattle."

"Who the hell was that on the other end of your phone, Moore?"

"I don't know. It was a woman's voice for sure. Unknown number, see?" as he showed his cell phone to Harris, "and she started the conversation by saying she was an anonymous caller that had important information about Crione Agency."

"Well, what do we do?"

"We get to that airport is what we do!"

The next morning Jacob and Naomi Willem left Will at home with Naomi's mother, Irene. They left for Seattle. Jacob insisted on seeing his dad one more time, telling Naomi she didn't have to come along, but he feared he would never see his father alive again. Naomi insisted on going. She confessed to Jacob exactly what she had done when we she left the other day. She confessed that she killed Frank Calister, and why. "He tried to kill me! He killed Rose . . . he was the one who invaded our home, Jacob. He is the tall man that Willem saw. He was going to kill you next," she stated to Jacob trying to justify her actions.

Jacob simply took her in his arms, and held her tight. "Everything will work out, my joy. I assure you. I will make all of this right. I am so sorry."

In the meantime, Detective Moore and Officer Harris had already staged themselves, along with a dozen other officers, a swat team, and airport police, where they awaited Richard Willem to show his face before attempting to board.

Detective Moore kept saying, "There is no chance we are going to allow this man passed security check point. There is no chance we're going to allow Richard Willem to leave the country. Someone must be held responsible for all of this, and I know in my gut that he is the man to hold the last pieces to this puzzle. With Richard Willem in custody, we can offer him safety, and he can lead us to Tommy Krindle."

"You're right, Boss, we almost have it all figured out, don't we?" Officer Harris smiled at Moore, feeling relieved this was almost over. "What a ride," she added.

Richard Willem was standing in line to pass through the security check point when he noticed what seemed to be too many police officers, more than normal. He knew something was wrong. He panicked, threw down his carryon luggage to the ground, and grabbed the woman in front of him. Pulling a gun from his bag on the floor, he pointed it at the woman's head, yelling aloud, "I am not responsible for Crione! I am not responsible for Crione!"

People panicked, scattered quickly from around him, some dropping to the floor from fear as the police officers and airport security all drew their guns upon Richard Willem, who was holding his hostage at gunpoint.

"Hold your fire!" Moore yelled out.

Jacob and Naomi Willem stood in silence as they entered the scene laid out in front of them. Jacob hurried in a limp towards his father, but Officer Harris quickly intersected him, knocking him to the ground.

"Richard Willem, you are under arrest! Put down your weapon!" Detective Moore called out.

Richards's eyes were full of desperation as he looked back at Naomi, then over to his son on the ground being held by the officer.

Jacob pleaded aloud to his father, "No . . . Dad, don't do it! Dad, please, just put down your gun . . . please." Huge tears welled up in his eyes.

So many guns were drawn on Richard, and the end of those barrels seemed to appear in 3D to him . . . his mind grew weary, his thoughts unclear.

"Release the woman, Richard. We know you are not responsible for Crione. We want to protect you. Now, put the gun on the ground, and place your hands in the air!" demanded Moore.

"Dad!" Jacob yelled out.

Officer Harris' arms stretched wide to keep Jacob, and Naomi who was now by his side, from going any closer.

Richard stared at his son, Jacob, as he let loose the woman he held hostage, and said aloud, "Son, I'm sorry." Richard Willem proceeded to point his gun squarely at the crowd of police.

The sound of gunshots immediately pierced through the airport, and Richards's lifeless body fell to the ground.

Suicide by police.

There was dramatic chaos all around, and it felt to Jacob and Naomi Willem like years had gone by before the noise calmed. Jacob sobbing in disbelief, and Naomi by his side doing her best to comfort him, they watched as police scurried to Richard Willem's body lying on the ground, and others going to attend the woman he had released from gunpoint.

Richard Willem's body was eventually bagged and taken away on a stretcher. The scene had cleared to only a few police officers left who were straightening up from the chaos, investigators taking pictures, and so on.

Detective Moore and Officer Harris told Jacob and Naomi Willem, after gaining their composure, that they had been through enough . . . they thanked them for their cooperation and sent them on their way home.

"Oh, just one more thing," Detective Moore called out to the Willems, "if you hear from Krindle . . ."

Naomi lifted her hand up in the air, palm facing Moore as if to tell him to say no more, stated, "Ya right, I'll call you."

CHAPTER 33

BEAUTIFUL IS LOVE

One Year Later: New York City.

Jacob and Naomi Willem left their bed to shower after passionate love making. The tenderness of their love for one another extended to the showering, as their passions for one another exploded with ecstasy.

"God, I have missed you," Jacob whispered in Naomi's ear. He held her tight as the shower water danced upon their skin, cleansing their past pains, and reassuring their unity. He never thought he could love her even more than before, realizing this wasn't a new found love as he never stopped loving her, but instead a new level of love. He'd never realized that was possible. He knew now more than ever before that he couldn't imagine his life without her. She made him feel whole. She made him want to be a better man.

"I have missed you, too, Baby. We are so blessed that you are doing so much better. Our new life here will be great. A new beginning, right?"

"Cheers to that," Jacob responded.

"Cheers to healing!" Naomi retorted delightfully.

They exchanged a kiss and another long embrace before exiting the shower to prepare for their day ahead.

"I am so excited that you and Willem will be with me tonight at the Gala. This will be the most exciting expose I have ever put on. Hundreds of people will be there to see my paintings. My work will finally be in the limelight, and you will never have to work again, if you don't want to."

"Well, it's been a year already. I guess I can get pretty used to it!" Jacob responded playfully.

"Our past is behind us now. All we have is our future. I love you so much, my husband."

"My Joy, my Naomi, my wife . . . I am so in love with you."

"See you tonight, then? Don't forget, 7 o'clock."

"Oh, how could I forget? We'll see you there!"

At the Gala, hundreds of people poured themselves onto the property, admiring Naomi's artwork. News crews were there filming the event, and paintings were being auctioned. Some purchased outright. It was a successful expose, indeed. Jacob Willem and Willem Carson, were Naomi's biggest fans, admiring her from afar, and small talking with the crowds of people. Naomi would often glance towards them, tossing a wink of her eye, or a mouthed "I love you guys" across the crowd.

As the evening came to a close, Naomi's crew was working on the cleanup. She, Jacob, and Willem, celebrated together as the last of the guests awaited their vehicles from the valet.

At a distance, Naomi thought she recognized a face waiting outside. She couldn't quite place it. "Who is that woman?" she asked Jacob while motioning towards the lady standing outside, looking in at them, and seemingly watching them closely.

"I'm not sure really. What do you think she is looking at? Us?"

Giggling a bit, Naomi decided, "Well, I guess I could just go say hello, couldn't I?"

Outside, Naomi did not need to approach the lady standing in the dark, because the lady was already walking towards Naomi herself. Naomi recognized her as soon as she hit the light.

What was Rachelle Wong, the Channel 7 News Anchor in northern Washington, doing here, Naomi asked herself.

"Naomi. Hello, again."

"Yes, hello. May I help you with something, Miss Wong?" she responded.

"Well, I've been following your work, your events, and shows, and what not. Beautiful Gala you had here tonight, Naomi."

"Thank you," Naomi's nerves growing quickly with discomfort. "Did you come all the way to New York just to compliment my work, Miss Wong?"

"Well, not exactly. I was hoping to talk with you if you have the time."

"Okay. Now?" Naomi asked.

"Yes, now. I want answers."

"And what sort of answers do you feel you are entitled to, Miss Wong? As I recall, you have quite the knack for barging in unwelcome to private events."

"Listen, Lady, I am sick of your games. I know what you did. And I know what your husband did, and his weasel of a father. I want answers as to where exactly my cameraman is. You know, a person, someone I worked with closely. He had a name, you know. Steve Maders. And he is still missing."

"I'm sorry, Rachelle, but I have no clue as to what you are even talking about. I'm afraid you have come a long ways to ask the wrong person the wrong questions."

"Naomi, I saw your husband in his truck leaving that mountain a year ago. That was right before we were suddenly being shot at, and Steve went missing. I can assume he has been murdered, but his family deserves closure. He's listed as a missing person. At least you were able to bury your friend."

"Are you suggesting my husband had something to do with your friend's disappearance?"

"I'm suggesting that you and your husband know more than you let on. And if you would just be honest, maybe some of this could come to an end finally. You do realize they are still looking for Tommy Krindle, don't you? His wife states that you know where he is."

"Tami? Don't waste your time with that woman. She is full of lies."

"Listen, Naomi. I was there the night of your husband's car accident. I was the one who gave the statement after that truck driver called 9-1-1. Do you realize that my other crew member died that night?"

"I had no idea. I'm . . . I'm sorry."

"Ya, a semi-truck barreled right in and over him. I had pieces of his shattered body all over me. Pieces of his organs and brain matted in my hair . . ."

"Rachelle, I didn't know. I'm sorry. What were you doing following my husband the night of his accident?"

"I wasn't following your husband. We were leaving the hospital when your husband almost hit us head-on."

"I really don't understand what it is you want from me, Rachelle. Really, I am sorry, but I must get back now."

"Naomi, my crew and I saw Jacob on Glacier Point Peak Pass that day. Then someone started shooting at us, some short scary guy that seemed to have vanished into thin air. Steve went missing; detectives are still searching for Tommy Krindle." Rambling quickly, Rachelle finally spelled it out to Naomi, "Listen, I believe Tommy Krindle is the man I saw in front of our news van that night when Steve Maders was murdered, and Joe Stanley was shot before being killed in that car accident which Jacob had caused. Everyone attached to Crione seems to either be dead, missing, or both, except for your husband.

Police don't have enough evidence to close the case much less do anything about it. I've been following their progress the entire time, and frankly, they aren't worth much. They barely gave a glance at my partner, Steve Maders, and the fact that he was murdered at Glacier Point Peak, because they say there's no proof. All they seem to be doing is filing search warrants for Tommy Krindle. And, if you ask me, I think Clint Borgam killed him and buried him in that tunnel, or worse.

I tell you, Naomi, I really don't give two shits about him, okay, he's the one who shot Steve, and he's the one who tried to kill me and my other partner, Joe Stanley. And now, here we are, a year later, and nothing has been resolved!

They let Jacob go, and I'm okay with that, except I know you both know more than you're telling anyone."

Naomi shook her head, waved her hands in the air showing her irritation with this rambling on. She interrupted Rachelle, "So, what is it exactly that you want now then? Are you here to bargain with me, blackmail, I don't get it. You've got nothing; that part, you have right, but what is it that you think you can get from me? What do you WANT?"

Rachelle responded sternly, "I want the truth."

"Miss Wong. Don't you get it? It seems to me that you already know the truth."

Jacob had been watching from inside the Gala during this conversation. He decided to walk out to greet them, to check on Naomi, as she appeared to be growing upset. Her glow from the exciting night had definitely dissipated.

Rachelle answered Naomi as she watched Jacob approaching them, "I want an exclusive from you . . . and from you, Jacob. I want to reveal the works of Crione Agency, detailing the involvement of Frank Calister, Tommy Krindle, Clint Borgam, and your father, Richard Willem to Glacier Point Peak Pass, the explosions, and nuclear warheads. This is my break, and I know enough to write the story whether you give me the facts I need or not."

Jacob looked at Naomi, and decided to intervene, "Miss Wong, if we agree to this, will you leave my family out of it? They have been through enough."

"This could focus the blame back on you, Jacob. Authorities will come questioning you again. They have been waiting for any clue to jump back on your case. Are you okay with that?"

"No, as a matter of fact, I am not. If I give you an exclusive, you cannot include my involvement in your story, whatsoever. You tell it how you must, but you have to agree that your story did not come from me or my wife. You agree to my terms, or no story."

"Agreed," Rachelle responded. She knew this was a risk, but she knew that even if she claimed her story to be speculation, that she still had one hell of a story. They set up a time to meet the next day over coffee.

During their meet the following day, Wong proceeded to question the Willems in detail. Jacob and Naomi both complied, offering her more details than she expected. She grew attached to their story; saw their genuine efforts in the choices they made. Amazed by their devotion to one another, to their family, and protecting one another, she swore to them her secrecy. There was no one left from Crione Agency except Jacob. "The only good, the only thing beautiful and pure that has come from any of this, is our marriage, my marriage to my devoted wife here," Jacob told Rachelle. "Crione is over. My work is over. But our love, our marriage, it has conquered all things evil. We only did what we felt was right at the time we were doing it. And we ended it, with our own two hands; we ended the evil doings of the world's largest nuclear and chemical weaponry exchange company."

Naomi added, "You see, even if our love and our actions had been questionable, it is a beautiful thing, our love. If we did not trust one another, it is possible that Jacob would be dead, and I would have thought he was responsible for all of this. I hope you see now that that is not the case."

Rachelle Wong did, indeed, write her news story, leaving the Willems directly out of the details. Her boss, Bob Milson released the story with Rachelle as the Primary Anchor-Woman less than a week after the return from her trip to New York City. Detective Charlie Moore and Officer Julie

Harris were waiting for her at her car when she left the news station that night. Rachelle's sworn secrecy, not to mention that she had developed a sincere connection with the Willems, stood her ground to protect her rights to conceal the identity of her sources. She told them, "For all I know, this is all hearsay."

Several years later Rachelle heard that the Willem's were vacationing in Massachusetts for a marathon that Jacob had been training for after his recovery was complete. It was during the *Boston bombings. Both Jacob and Naomi were amongst the ones killed in the explosions that day.

Their son, Willem Carson, then and now an adult, returned to their New York home, truly alone. It is believed that he has changed his identity, and that he, too, has become an artist.

Shortly after the death of her fondly looked upon murderous acquaintances, Jacob and Naomi Willem, Rachelle Wong released a book, naming it:

Beautiful Is Love,
The Real Story Behind Glacier Point Peak Pass

The end.

ACKNOWLEDGMENTS AND REFERENCES:

Author's statement: "I would like to acknowledge the tools, references, and people that have helped me throughout my research for this project prior to publication."

1. Many kudos and deep appreciation to my husband, Doug Harrison for his wit, research assistance, critique, and influence throughout the development and progress of this project's entirety.

2. To Molly Adams, I extend sincere gratitude for your honest feedback and suggestions during the final revisions. To Jessica Mitchell, I thank you for continuous encouragement. My undying gratitude extends to Glenda Jorgensen, for your critique, encouragement, and editorial expertise. I would also like to acknowledge my appreciation to Mary Anaya, Emily Simmons, Jim Thomsen, Marcie Dillard, Ron Reust, and Lonnie Moon.

3. Preface: Old Market, Omaha, the premier arts and entertainment district in downtown Omaha, per "Entertainment District" on www.oldmarket.com/

4. Chapter 1: Job titles for the Willems' science backgrounds were obtained and inspired by and through online researching; i.e.: Wikipedia and Google results

5. Documentary Title: Tapped, Released: 2009 by Atlas Films, by Co-director, Writer & Editor: Jason Lindsey, Producer/Director: Stephanie Soechtig, and Executive Producer: Michael Walrath, Description: "Tapped examines the role of the bottled water industry and its effects on our health, climate change, pollution and our reliance on oil."

6.   Chapter 6: Google population search 2011, Darrington, WA

7.   Chapter 6: Google population search 2011, Whitehorse/OSO, WA

8.   Chapter 6: MIT is the abbreviation for Massachusetts Institute of Technology, a private college located in Cambridge, Massachusetts. [2011 Wikipedia definition: "MIT has five schools and one college, containing a total of 32 academic departments, with a strong emphasis on scientific and technological education and research. Founded in 1861 in response to the increasing industrialization of the United States, the institute adopted the European polytechnic university model and emphasized laboratory instruction from an early date . . ."]

9.   Chapter 9: Artist: Bob Dylan, Album: [Columbia Records Presents] The Essential Bob Dylan, Song Title: The Answers Are Blowing In The Wind

10. Chapter 30: Artist: Stevie Ray Vaughan, Album: In Step, Song Title: Walking A Tight Rope

11. *a gray, "Gy," is a unit of radiation dose absorbed by matter

12. *Boston Marathon bombings. April 15th 2013; Wikipedia, states two pressure cooker bombs exploded, killing 3 people and injuring an estimated 264 others. The bombs exploded about 13 seconds and 210 yards apart, near the finish line on Boylston Street.